THE RAVEN

Supernatural Stories

Part 1

By Ellie LaCrosse

THE BOOK CHIEF®

IGNITE YOUR WRITING

Published by The Book Chief Publishing House 2024
(a trademark under Lydian Group Ltd)
Suite 2A, Blackthorn House, St Paul's Square,
Birmingham, B3 1RL
www.thebookchief.com

ISBN: 978-1-0686981-4-9

Book Cover Design: Claire Gardner / Deearo Marketing
Editing: Sharon Brown
Typesetting / Proofreading: Sharon Brown
Publishing: Sharon Brown

Published by The Book Chief

Table of Contents

DEDICATION 5

PROLOGUE 7

1 9

    MESSENGERS OF THE FORGOTTEN............................. 9
    Ellie LaCrosse.. 9

2 27

    LUCKY 27
    F. Taylor 27

3 47

    A SPECTRE CALLS 47
    Jo A. Ripley 47

4 65

    PEIL ISLAND 65
    Dorothy King.. 65

5 71

    THE UNWELCOME GUEST 71
    Pamela Edwards 71

6 77

    THE HOUSE THAT WASN'T THERE 77
    Margaret Martindale 77

7 85

    A RAVEN FREED: A STORY OF TWO WORLDS 85
    Laura Billingham 85

8 101

    THE RAVEN GEOMANCER.................................... 101
    Ellie LaCrosse.. 101

9 .... **111**

    DEATH'S DOOR 111
      Margaret Martindale *111*

10 .... **115**

    OCEANS APART 115
      Julie Gibson *115*

11 .... **131**

    A TALE FROM THE TREETOP: RAVENS AND MONKS 131
      Fiona Pervez *131*
    THE VALE OF THE DEADLY NIGHTSHADE 136
      Fiona Pervez *136*
    THE MURDER 140
      Fiona Pervez *140*

12 .... **149**

    THE SHADOW MAN 149
      Marjorie Dearn *149*

ACKNOWLEDGEMENTS **161**

ABOUT THE AUTHORS **163**

    LEAD AUTHOR - ELLIE LACROSSE 164
    JULIE GIBSON 165
    FIONA PERVEZ 166
    MARGARET MARTINDALE 167
    LAURA BILLINGHAM 168
    DOROTHY KING 169
    PAMELA EDWARDS 170
    JO A. RIPLEY 171
    MARJORIE DEARN 172
    F. TAYLOR 173

Dedication

To the 'Secret Squirrel Coven'

You know who you are x

Prologue

Supernatural tales of the unexplainable have always captivated me and countless others. They are a constant, eerie presence—faint noises in the night, fleeting shadows across the room, flickering lights, strange smells, and objects mysteriously moving or falling. While my mind instinctively seeks a logical, scientific explanation, I'm often intrigued by the question, "What if it can't be explained?"

The raven, a powerful symbol in mythology and folklore, often embodies a dark, romantic supernatural character, reinforcing humanity's fascination with the unknown. Some of these stories delve into the raven's mysterious traits—its intelligence, chatter, memory, and almost telepathic nature. In literature and film, the raven has long been portrayed as a harbinger of doom, death, and the eternal struggle between good and evil.

A lone raven chattering nearby can send chills down your spine, a feeling explored throughout these tales. Each story is crafted to make you wonder, "What if these events were real?" Prepare to be entertained and unnerved, as these original supernatural stories leave you questioning the line between the natural and the inexplicable.

Ellie LaCrosse

1

Messengers of the Forgotten

Ellie LaCrosse

The Scots raiders came down from the North. The town had been subjected to lightning raids with scary clansmen on horseback. They attacked during early dawn when the crimson morning streaks in the sky matched the vermillion pools of blood left in their wake.

The borderlands were wild, and Mercia, where the English King and his court resided, seemed remote to the Cumberland landowners and townsfolk. The Furness peninsula on the northwestern coastline had been raided the year before. Robert de Brus's warriors plundered the mined iron ore to create steel for their weapons.

The gibbet had been erected under instruction from the Abbot, Humfrei de Voil, in addition to an extra thin standing chamber; the oubliette dug out from the bottom of the small dungeon in the Pele Tower. Humfrei felt he had to hold the line against the annoying terrorists that thieved cattle, cash and corn, especially when famine struck. He wasn't going to allow insurrection, sacking and pillaging of his town. He was confident the archers guarding the ramparts would defend adequately.

He kept ravens as messengers between the Abbey and the tower, which was only a short distance away. They were unerringly accurate in their tidings when the raiders were approaching. They were also good spies, as they could mimic human speech patterns, words, and snippets of conversations. He kept them well fed; he didn't want them captured and spilling all of *his* conversations!

The rotting corpses in the gibbet were the harbingers of doom and destruction. The message would get back to the thieving scum, and he'd kidnap one of their leaders and throw them into the oubliette in the tower. They would either serve a ransom, or they'd die horribly where they stood, completely neglected and forgotten.

When life quietened down several years later in the borderlands, the trap door to the oubliette had been sealed. No one enquired or bothered to retrieve any entombed corpse if, indeed, there had ever been anyone unlucky enough to face this medieval torture.

However, the one enemy the town could not defeat eerily descended through a bale of woollen cloth jumping with fleas. The traders and townsfolk alike had heard tales of plagues sweeping up from the south and further across Europe. They had rules about quarantining goods for a month before market. Unfortunately, this bale of fine cloth was wanted by a noblewoman, and she paid a servant to fetch it sooner.

Inevitably, the town was ravaged by the 'Black Death'. A huge plague pit was dug on the edge of the settlement near the Pele Tower. The swollen, bloody, cadaverous stench reeked under the nostrils of the townsfolk. Many succumbed to the ghastly buboes, fever, vomiting and coughing. Not realising each cough sprayed annihilation to others in close proximity. Whole families perished, but eventually, the plague fizzled out, and the survivors struggled with their apocalyptic reality.

There were not enough able-bodied men to farm their tithes. Within a few short years, the town fell into ruin, and the land was not cultivated. They realised that instead of paying higher wages, the town was sacrificed to the production of sheep. The serfs' hovels and town buildings were cleared and razed to the ground. Over time, the scattered crumbling stonework was covered in moss and earth.

Even the Pele Tower, vital for the town's defence, eventually became too expensive to upkeep and maintain. It rotted and decayed, and its dressed stonework was stolen until many centuries later, the mound was covered in grass and vegetation. The sheep had destroyed what the elements hadn't eroded with time with their grinding and benign trampling. Humans or Herbivores? The Abbots made their choice and grew rich in the woollen trade and meat supply.

No one remembered the town; no tower stood sentinel; it had all been forgotten…

In the following millennium, the sheep had been pushed further back into the surrounding fells, and the land yielded to the march of modernity and creeping progress. After WW2, returning soldiers and their families needed homes.

Once again, the area had been built upon, but interestingly, it was not the elevated craggy mound where the tower once stood. Modern brick council homes for the quarrymen and railway workers, later the pickers and packers required for the distribution centres.

On the edge of The Lakes, it was a quiet, settled, and peaceful corner of the northwest. Close enough to the Cumbrian coastline's stunning beauty and magnificent mountains, it was a desirable place to settle, and the town once more grew and prospered.

Sam and her partner Andy drove around the area looking at potential new homes. They were debating whether to invest in a new starter home on the edge of the town or go for something more traditional, a 'do-er-upper'. Andy favoured getting stuck into some DIY after years of shared digs and not being able to hang wallpaper. Sam wanted a fresh start—a blank canvas where no one had lived before.

After a frustrating morning of having to be polite to potential vendors and seeing some mis-described near derelict homes, Sam persuaded Andy to swing by a new development on the outskirts of town. It was in a slightly elevated position and had a newly completed show house. The site plans were seductively colour-coded, showing the development's phased progress.

"The site is in a slightly raised position next to the old iron ore workings near the town", the charming site negotiator explained.

"Oh, okay, is there a mining survey to look at?"

"It's not been mined for centuries, and the site isn't over the old workings. It's just the quirky geology of this area; at least, it's well above the water table here."

"I love the views. When are you releasing the next homes for sale?"

"A deposit will secure your plot, and we'll honour the prices shown in the brochure, even if prices rise in the next phase."

Andy swallowed hard. He knew Sam; she'd made up her mind already. He looked at her shining eyes. He loved her and wanted this to be their first home together to raise a longed-for family. He wasn't paying a deposit today; he'd make her work for it. She could treat him to lunch!

As they drove out of the site onto the road towards the heart of the town, something caught Andy's eye as they passed a quaint stone-fronted primary school. Sam had asked him to slow down so she could get a feel for its proximity to the new development. Thankfully, Sam hadn't seen the mature oak tree standing in the background of the playground. It was only a split-second view, but it made Andy feel startled. On several of the lower branches were hanging dead ravens. Their necks were grotesquely angled, and their iridescent plumage ruffled in the breeze. Four black shapes swinging like on a gibbet. He blinked about to point it out, but there was nothing. The images had disappeared. It had unnerved him. He was probably low on blood sugar and needed food!

By the end of lunch, they had discussed all the pros and cons of buying a new home. They had been prepared; after years of saving hard and sorting out a mortgage-in-principle, they were good to go.

Mary Tait was the Chair of the 'Tidy-Town' and 'Britain in Bloom Committee'. She made it her business to 'fix' the odd town planter, constantly weeding and infilling spring bulbs, whipping out a plastic carrier scrunched in her warm gilet for litter picks and having copious amounts of tea and cake planning a winning planting scheme season by season.

She sometimes popped into the local primary school, just on the outskirts of town, to volunteer reading to the pre-schoolers. Her daughter was Head, which was a way of contributing to her community. She was a dependable and stout supporter of anything related to the town she loved.

It was late autumn, and she felt an ice blast coming over the fells; as she turned up her coat collar, she heard the wind rustling through the dying oak leaves, which were always the last leaves to fall off the trees. She loved the childish pleasure of walking through piles of dry leaves and hearing them scrunch and crackle underfoot. The twilight sky had dark orange criss-crosses that illuminated the outstretched limbs of the old oak. It clearly revealed a group of swinging dead ravens strung around the lower branches. She screamed at the grotesque vision.

The Police were called. Mary's statement was taken, the scene surveyed, photos snapped, and dead ravens bagged up for evidence. Mary had nightmares and recounted this menacing image to her 'Tidy-Town' crowd over slabs of chocolate brownie and lattes in the town's latest coffee shop.

"How frightful! Good job, the kiddies didn't spot them; they could have traumatised them for life!"

"It's an old country thing, isn't it?"

"Folklore, mi dad used to string up crows to keep the buggers from pecking the seeds in the fields...clever birds...all of 'em, crows, ravens, intelligent like. Mi' dad said they could talk to each other, warn each other to clear off!"

"Urgh, why would anyone do it next to a school? Sickos, people are moving into the town, bringing some undesirable types around here!"

"I bet it's a farmer or someone local, not a newbie."

Over the following months, several sightings of strung-up ravens were reported hanging from lamp-posts, roundabout signage, road bollards and several trees around the new housing development. Questions started to be raised at the town council meetings after a local reporter wrote an expose and photographed a hanging raven.

"Cllr. Dixon, you wanted to give the meeting an update on these disgusting acts of Corvids being strung up around town?"

"Er, yes, I've had an update from our Community Police Officer who has logged several incidents around the town with large birds, mostly ravens, being strung up and tied to various objects around the town."

"Who on earth would do that? Is there any CCTV footage?" asked the Town Clerk.

"Don't be daft, it's not bloody 'Crime Watch'!"

"A countryman or *woman,* don't you think? Can't imagine a young oik doing it."

"But to what end?"

"It's likely a message to bugger off, keep away; someone doesn't like the new development?"

"Well, patrols are being stepped up around the primary school lane and the main road leading to the new development. Hopefully, now that it's been reported that they've made their protest, it'll stop. Bit macabre though, and not good for our town's image!" Cllr. Dixon huffed and closed his notebook.

Sam and Andy finally had the keys to their new home after a fraught few months getting through conveyancing. They spent an exhausting weekend hauling packing cases to various rooms and making some rooms at least cosy. Tired but blissfully happy, they slept soundly in their new bed, brand-new home, and a new housing estate. It was just what Sam wanted, and even Andy had to admit that he felt very settled and 'adult'. Over the following weeks, they even got a Christmas tree and were looking forward to spring when they would tackle the new garden.

"It's pretty mild for December; I might have a prod about in the garden and get some of the crap out of the builder's topsoil; bloke at work told me to get my spade out and give it the once over before laying turf. He found loads of builder stuff, rubbish, and broken bricks. Then, after Christmas, we'll measure up and plan the garden. It's great that we've got a mature oak tree on the plot. It was one of the reasons for picking this site, I think we struck it lucky!"

"Oh, get you, Mr Domestic, so we've already settled the division of labour in this relationship, have we? Me indoors, you protector of the perimeter?" Sam giggled.

"Ha, ha, ha, very funny. It's simply a case of blue jobs and pink jobs."

"So, no purple jobs then?"

"Come here, you daft mare, and give us a kiss!"

As Andy sidled up to Sam for a smooch, there was a loud cacophony of 'cawing" sounds.

"What the heck is that?"

They both opened the patio door out to the garden and froze on the spot as they saw many ravens circling the oak tree. Their sound was very strange; it was like they were chattering.

"Oubli! Oubli! Oubli! Oubli! Oubli!"

"Ette! Ette! Ette! Ette! Ette!"

"Oubliette! Oubliette! Oubliette! Oubliette!

Sam screeched, and Andy ran out to protect her, flapping his arms wildly above his head. Dark forms swooshed and swept past the roof of the house and back to the tree. Then suddenly they all fell silent.

Both just stood still, their heart beating wildly. It was very weird and alarming. Then Andy turned to Sam and said, "Quick! Get inside!"

In no time at all, the first 'thud' on the patio window was followed by constant cawing and what seemed like a beak tapping on the windows of the house facing the garden. Sam started to cry, "What's going on? Oh, I don't like this, it's creepy!"

"Sam, there's something I should have told you. Hear me out: after our first visit to the site earlier in the year, as we drove past the school, I thought I saw some dead ravens strung up by the oak tree next to the school."

Sam was wide-eyed, "Ravens, those friggin' big black things that are outside our window?"

"I thought I was just hungry and seeing shite. Look, this is a little dismaying I'm sure it's a strange north country thing. I dunno, I'm not a country bloke!"

"Dismaying? These bloody birds are terrorising me in my garden; call the Police!"

"Listen, Sam; it's stopped; the tapping has stopped."

Silence. Andy gingerly opened the patio door, banged on the garden light, and promptly shouted, "Oh Christ!" As a solitary raven magnificently revealed in the moonlight, its oily, midnight black plumage shimmering and its neck swivelling towards the couple, squawked, "Oubliette!" and flew off.

Sam scrambled to open a packing case for a bottle of scotch. After both had taken a swig to calm their nerves, Sam grabbed her phone.

"What was that sound they were making? It sounded French. Obi-sommat?"

"Oubliette"

"Okay, Mr. Google, What's O-U-B-L-I-E-T-T-E?"

"Something that is forgotten. A secret dungeon with access through a trapdoor in its ceiling. Victims in oubliettes were often left to starve and dehydrate to death. Medieval torture."

"Call the Police, Andy, CALL THE POLICE!"

The call was logged, and the Community Police Officer was booked to call in to discuss the alarming event.

The young couple were understandably rattled but agreed that they lived in a semi-rural location and were not used to being in the same proximity to wildlife. When they recounted the event, they did feel a bit silly; however, the young local Police Officer was professional and reassuring, saying that there had been a rise in raven sightings. She had never heard of the word 'Oubliette' but would ask at the station and do some research. She omitted to mention that some ravens had been found strung up around the town recently, as she felt their nerves were already shredded.

Christmas came and went, and the young couple settled into their new community. No more ravens came visiting, not even to roost in the oak tree, and gradually, the light returned. The evenings got milder, and spring arrived as a welcome friend.

They hadn't yet heard directly from the young P.O., but she had left an answerphone message to say she was trying to contact a Medieval History specialist at Lancaster University. They thought the region had been settled hundreds of years ago, but no one locally knew anything.

Sam suddenly reminded Andy to get his spade out one particularly mild weekend.

"Ey up, love. I'm hoping to get a basic garden for the Easter holiday. Are you going to clear up the tip outside for us?"

"Anything for you, taskmaster!" He giggled.

Andy had toiled all of Saturday to till the topsoil. Over several hours and copious cups of tea, he'd managed to rake and dig out a collection of builder swag and debris piled up in his wheelbarrow. Old coke tins, sandwich wrappers, broken bricks, small sections of reinforcing ties, rusty nails. He was looking forward to having a long relaxing soak, watching a bit of footy on the T.V. and a cuddle from Sam when his spade connected with something firm.

"Heck! What the?" he exclaimed, quite astonished when his spade got wedged under a huge stud-like forged nail.

"Sam! Sam! Come out here; I've found something strange!"

"Are you okay? What's the matter?" She replied breathily, peering over his spade.

"There's something underneath this bit of metal…look… it's making a sort of clonking sound, listen, it's sort of hollow sounding?"

"Is it a box? Buried treasure?" she giggled. "Oh, go on, Andy, find us some loot!"

Ten minutes later, Andy had scrapped the topsoil off an area about 50cm in diameter, which looked like a grid of metal with studs in it.

"I think it's been there a while. There may have been some wooden slats or something underneath the grid. Well, I'm pooped, I'm done in, I'll look at it again in the morning, I've done enough digging for one day, and the light's fading fast; it'll be dark very soon!"

With that, he did one last dig, and suddenly, the metal grid broke through. In an effort not to lose the spade; he stumbled, and his leg slid into the opening, but he grazed his shin on the protruding metal, with blood trickling and soaking through his jeans.

"Ow! That hurts…Oh, Bloody Hell…Help me Sam!"

Before Sam had time to react, several ravens swooped over to Andy and mob-pestered him, cawing "Oubliette!", "Oubliette!" over and over and over.

Sam screamed, but still, they dived and swooped, cawing the word "OUBLIETTE!" even louder.

"Andy! I'm going to get my phone and call the Police. Can you wave your arms about to scare off the birds?"

"Quick! Go on!" he shouted, but no sooner had he waved his arms than he completely slipped through the broken metal grid, wailing as he fell straight down a hole in the ground.

A terrifying, blood-curdling scream that didn't even sound human.

The oubliette had swallowed him like some diabolical orifice, and the raven's warnings were unheeded.

Who else had known that the *'forgotten'* still had a tale to tell?

2

Lucky

F. Taylor

Black cats were always interchangeable with Naomi. The shelter where she worked got so many of them that they blurred into one creature. They seemed to melt into the shadows, forgotten as quickly as they had come—all except for one.

Her name was Lucky, which was probably a joke, considering black cats' reputation. Naomi was used to hearing odd sounds or dealing with strange behaviour from the cats—after all, many of them had come from rough backgrounds before ending up at the shelter. She could handle cats fighting, scratching, and screaming. What freaked her out the most was that Lucky didn't make any sound.

Laura, one of the other workers at the shelter, was convinced Lucky was injured or was born mute, but a visit to the vets showed no signs of internal damage of any kind. Lucky was a perfectly healthy adult cat. Odd. But she wasn't aggressive, and space was limited, so she was put into a pen with two other adult female cats. They avoided her like the plague. The older cats were always a little wary of newcomers, so Naomi didn't think anything of it. But the weeks passed, and the other cats still didn't want to interact with her, nor did Lucky seem to want anything to do with them or the workers at the shelter. The other cats would hiss at Naomi or at one of her co-workers whenever they held Lucky or paid her any particular attention. They would huddle together in one corner of the pen, watching with wide, glowing eyes as Lucky prowled in front of the gate.

"There's just something weird about her," Naomi said, her eyes fixed on Lucky.

Jake huffed a laugh as he bent to put away a box of cat litter.

"You're the *only* one who thinks that." Laura rolled her eyes and kicked her legs, sending her swivel chair into a lazy spin.

"She just has a menacing vibe"

"A menacing *vibe*?" Jake straightened up and leant his head around the corner to peer at her, "She's a cat. She's a very well-behaved cat, considering the circumstances. Isn't that the opposite of a menacing vibe?"

"What circumstances? I thought you didn't know how she ended up here?" Laura asked, turning to him, her chair squeaking in protest.

He shrugged, "It's a shelter. Animals don't end up in shelters for happy reasons, do they? Usually, someone died, or they're being neglected."

Laura made a face at him.

"What? It's true. The point is, just be glad she's not tipping over the litter tray every five minutes or fighting with the other inmates."

"I guess." Naomi glanced over at Lucky again, frowning.

"Don't worry," Laura said, "She's a pretty girl; she'll get adopted like *That*." She snapped her fingers to emphasise her point.

Laura was right. Lucky was adopted quickly.

A young woman came in looking for a cat that would play well with her existing pet. Her original cats, Cinnamon and Ginger, had come as a pair from a litter, but Ginger had been put down a couple of weeks ago. Not wanting Cinnamon to get lonely, she was looking for a friendly adult cat to keep her company. Naomi attempted to steer her towards some of their slightly older cats who had been at the shelter for a while, but she took to Lucky like a duck to water and agreed to take her by the end of the week if she got along well with Cinnamon.

Jake supervised Lucky on her playdate and laughed at Naomi when she nervously asked him how it went.

"Menacing vibe, my arse. Those two were playing like kittens. Perhaps it's just the shelter that makes her unfriendly."

Lucky was gone by Friday. Naomi watched the sweet young woman pack her away into the back seat of her car with dread pooling in her stomach.

By Monday morning, she was back. The woman, Andy, had gotten into a car wreck over the weekend, and her adorable two-door car had been crushed against a lorry on the motorway. She was pronounced dead at the scene. Her cats came to the shelter. Cinnamon was a black and brown calico with a distinct patch of white fur over the left eye. As soon as she was placed in a pen with Lucky, she started swiping and hissing at her, her claws out. The budding friendship that Jake had described was nowhere to be found. This wasn't playfighting either- on one especially vicious pass, Cinnamon managed to draw blood. In retaliation, Lucky gave a scratch of her own, and the situation devolved from there. Eventually, the two had to be separated permanently. When Cinnamon was put with others, all of her aggressive behaviour stopped, aside from the odd bit of hissing over food, and she became a perfectly calm cat. Lucky, too, went back to her usual stoicism and the other cats she was placed with avoided her, just as they had before.

Soon, another family came in looking to adopt. The father was a handsome lawyer, with only a few early wrinkles beginning to appear around his dark eyes. His wife was an estate agent who walked in on staggeringly tall heels, her face hidden behind a pair of large sunglasses. Their son couldn't have been older than eight, still clutching a cuddly toy and clinging to his mother's arm. When he grinned, Naomi saw that his two front teeth were missing. In an uncharacteristic show of friendliness, Lucky nuzzled the boy's hand and gracefully wove between the mother's legs. Naomi frowned but let it go. The family were content to take her, and when their background check came back clean, Naomi was more than happy to see the back of Lucky. Hopefully, this time, it will be for good.

"That's so weird." Jake looked over Laura's shoulder at the TV screen in the reception area. It was showing the local news.

"I mean, they were so normal. They seemed normal, right?" he looked at Naomi questioningly.

She shook her head. "Sound's suspicious to me. I mean, you hear of this kind of thing on, y'know, Midsummer Murders. You never think it happens to real people."

"Police are saying murder-suicide. They think the dad went crazy. Stress at work, probably, and just BAM!" Jake clapped his hands in emphasis, "Whole family, gone."

"That's horrible." Laura covered her mouth with her hand, "How could anyone do something like that? And the kid too-"she gestured wildly, her eyes glistening with tears. "The cat! What happened to Lucky?"

"She's fine. The Police will bring her over later once they lock down the whole scene. I got a call this morning," Jake said without looking away from the TV.

"Oh, that's a relief." Laura sighed.

"What? A guy completely loses his marbles, kills his family and then offs himself, and you're worried about a CAT?" Naomi snapped, glaring at Laura.

"What? It's not her fault! The poor thing must be terrified."

"I don't know; adding a new pet is a lot of stress; it might've tipped dear old Dad over the edge." Jake tilted his head in thought.

"Come off it, you don't believe that, do you?" Laura crossed her arms and frowned. She seemed so much smaller than the others from her usual spot in the reception's swivel chair.

"' Course not, I'm just messing with you." Jake gave her a lopsided grin, his blonde hair falling into his eyes.

"Well, I'm not! I'm telling you guys, there's something off about that cat. Surely, you noticed the complete change in how she acted as soon as that family paid attention to her.

She was never that affectionate with us, and we've been bringing her food twice a day for three months." Naomi protested.

"So?" Jake looked at her sceptically, one eyebrow raised.

"So, have you *ever* seen a cat act like that? It's weird!"

"All right, I'll admit, it's a little weird, but don't you think you're reading too much into this? What are you gonna do, accuse a cat of murder?" Jake snorted.

"And the car crash?" Naomi continued, unperturbed.

"What about the car crash? It could happen to anyone." Laura flicked her ponytail over her shoulder.

"I wish it would happen to *you*." Jake laughed. Laura threw a pencil at him in retaliation.

"I think-"Naomi tried again.

"Ugh! Drop it, will you!" Laura interrupted, rolling her eyes. "Coincidences happen. For example, when my aunt went on holiday to Egypt, the person in the room next to her was from." The phone rang, interrupting her. Before long, both Jake and Laura moved on to other tasks, leaving Naomi to cover reception.

But try as she might, Naomi couldn't leave it alone. The odds of both sets of Lucky's most recent owners dying in such a short space of time was just too big of a coincidence for her to ignore. For the next couple of hours, she scrolled through local news and Facebook posts, eyes peeled for any mention of a silent, black cat.

Eventually, her search paid off. A local woman, Debbie, posted about her mother's missing black cat nearly five months ago. Naomi dropped her a message, saying a cat matching her description had been dropped off at their shelter. Upon being sent a photo of Lucky, which Naomi pulled from the shelter's website, Debbie confirmed that that was her mother's cat. She asked Debbie to come down to the shelter so that they could double-check and make any updates to Lucky's records. Debbie agreed and came down at lunchtime.

"Great!" Naomi plastered on a fake smile, "That's one mystery solved; at least, we were all wondering where she'd come from. You want her back, I assume?"

"Good God, no!" Debbie looked horrified at the very idea. "Not a cat person?" Naomi asked, her smile faltering just a little.

"Not especially, no. But even if I *was*", she looked at Lucky disdainfully, her lip curling, "You couldn't pay me to have that thing in my house."

"Huh?" Naomi frowned in confusion. "I know black cats have a bit of a spooky reputation, but…"

"I mean it," Debbie said, completely serious. "Three owners down, and she always seemed to, uh, well, land on her feet. I'm not superstitious or anything, but that cat gives me the heebie-jeebies." She shuddered and turned to go.

"Wait, what do you mean three owners down?" Naomi reached out to stop Debbie from leaving.

"Lucky's first owner was an older woman. I forget her name. She wasn't fond of vets' bills or paperwork, which is probably why you didn't have Lucky in your system. I don't know where she got Lucky from. She may have just lured her in off the street with a can of tuna." Debbie shrugged, her eyes sliding back to Lucky uneasily. "Regardless, Lucky found herself with a new owner quite quickly because that old bat popped her clogs. Then, the same thing happened to the neighbour Lucky was passed on to. And then another. They all lived on the same street in a retirement complex, and Lucky was simply passed on whenever one of them died. If anyone else found it suspicious that all three women died within the space of less than two months, no one said anything."

"Yeah, but people die in those places all the time, right? And you said they were old."

"Not that old. Certainly, the last two weren't. They were in good health, and then that thing…" Debbie points at Lucky with one manicured finger, "enters the house, and suddenly ambulances get called in the middle of the night, and I've got another funeral to go to."

"My Mum ended up in that retirement place, just in time to become unlucky owner number four. She felt bad for it, I suppose. I made her take it to the vet to get it checked for fleas and whatever else. She named it 'Lucky' because it had outlived so many damn owners." Debbie rolled her eyes.

"Wow." Naomi blinked owlishly at her. "And your mum, did she- uh, is she all right?"

"She died about a week later. Everyone said it was the stress of the move or being exposed to so many new germs all at once, but it was just too weird. When I went to clear out Mum's things, the cat wasn't there, and to be honest, I really couldn't care less what happened to it. Maybe some part of me hoped it had been squashed under a car. I felt bad about it later, though, so I made the post, not expecting anything to come of it." She shook her head.

"Sorry for dragging you down here then." Naomi tried to smile again, but it felt weak.

"It's fine." Debbie made a dismissive gesture. She looked like she wanted to leave.

"Here, let me walk you out," Naomi said half-heartedly as she said goodbye to Debbie at the door. Her mind was reeling, and she was in a daze for the rest of the day. After she dropped her third box of kitty litter, Jake sent her home early. She heard him grumble as he grabbed a broom to sweep the mess.

The next day, Naomi woke up late for her shift and scrambled to get ready. When she was halfway out the door, her phone buzzed angrily at her. She answered it.

"Jake! I know I'm late: I'll be like ten minutes."

"Can you check in on Laura on your way in? You guys live near each other, right? She was supposed to be there an hour ago, but she's not answering her phone."

"Uh, yeah, yeah, I can do that. Maybe she's just sick today?"

"Yeah, probably, or hungover. Either way, she took Lucky home with her last night and…"

"Wait, what? Why?" Naomi stopped dead in the middle of the street, wide-eyed.

"She was making a fuss, throwing up hairballs and vomiting all afternoon. You must have missed it when you were hiding in the storeroom. And you know how Laura is, soft as a feather, so she started getting all weepy and begged to take Lucky home to keep an eye on her. I was dying for a smoke, and she just kept going on and on about it, so I said she could just to shut her up."

"Jake!" Naomi yelled down the phone at him. "You know that's not allowed! Management is gonna have your head!"

"Shut up, shut up, I know, okay?" he snapped back. "Just check on her, alright? It's not like she doesn't answer her phone; it's usually glued to her hand. At the very least, bring Lucky back here."

"Fine." Naomi snapped and hung up. She legged it to Laura's house. They lived not too far away—a ten-minute walk, which she knew she could reduce to five if she cut through a public footpath.

The path was overgrown and shaded by trees, but it was quiet, and sunlight filtered through the gaps in the leaves overhead. A small stream ran beside it, the gently trickling water at complete odds with Naomi's rising panic as she dialled and re-dialled Laura's number. It kept going to voicemail.

Finally, she made it to Laura's house. From the outside, everything looked normal. The square, red-bricked building looked a little shabby, but no more than usual. Laura's car was even still parked on the street outside. Naomi rang the doorbell, but no one answered, so she knocked on the front door. It swung open under her hand.

"Laura?" she called, her voice echoing in the empty house. She stepped inside. "Laura, are you there?" The hallway, living room, and kitchen were empty. She froze as she returned to the corridor and prepared to go upstairs.

Laura was lying in a crumpled heap at the bottom of the stairs. She was lying face up in a pool of her own blood, her face white and staring blankly at the ceiling. Lucky sat perched on her chest, her head bent, her tiny pink tongue lapping at the blood that spilt out of Laura. The cat's entire mouth was red with still-warm blood; droplets of it slid down her whiskers and splattered over Laura's chest. Lucky paused and looked up at Naomi.

Shelter work meant she wasn't particularly squeamish; Lord knows she had seen enough cats in poor condition to give her a strong stomach. But the sight of this *thing* eating her friend's corpse turned her stomach. Her hands flew to cover her mouth in shock. She could have sworn that the cat grinned at her.

Suddenly, she was enraged. Jake could laugh all he wanted, but this cat had been killing its owners; Naomi was sure of it. So many deaths in such a short time wasn't normal, and here was the proof! Laura wasn't a clumsy girl; she wasn't a frail old woman who easily tripped down the stairs. Besides, cats didn't eat humans unless they were starving, and Naomi had seen Lucky's food bowl still full of dry food in the kitchen. The damned thing had wanted to do it.

Naomi seized Lucky by the scruff of her neck and took off out of the house. The beast scratched and bit at her the entire way, drawing bloody scratches across Naomi's hands and arms. She refused to let go. She was half out of her mind with anger, grief and indignation. How *dare* this tiny little thing cause such pain and misery to so many people?

They were back on that deserted footpath. Naomi raised Lucky high over her head and threw her with all her might down, down, down over the small hill and into the stream beyond. Her head hit the ground with a sickening CRUNCH. Lucky's body lay heavily in the water, the current curving around it. Blood bloomed as if someone had thrown a bunch of carnations into the water, only to get washed away as the stream flowed downhill. No breath stirred Lucky's chest.

Naomi was panting, sweat cooling on her flushed skin, pasting her hair to her forehead. She had no intention of going back into the house, but she waited outside for the ambulance crew to arrive. They spoke to her, and she answered their questions in a daze, only startling back to life when her phone buzzed in her pocket. Drawing it out, she saw that it was sticky with blood and that her hands had been stained red, too.

It was Jake calling to check up on her. That was enough for the dam to burst. She sobbed down the phone, saying that Laura was dead, that there had been some kind of accident, that she was waiting while the ambulance took away her body. Through his shock, Jake reassured her that he would phone Laura's parents, whose number was on file at the shelter.

"But where's Lucky?" He asked.

"What?" she replied dumbly, wiping tears from her face with the back of her hand. The action left a smear of blood on her cheek.

"The cat. Lucky. Laura took her home last night. Did you see her?"

"No." she lied, her voice watery. "No, but the door was open; maybe she got out."

The rest of what Jake said was lost on her. Something about taking the day off. Naomi was more than happy to do that. She went home and cried in the shower until the water went cold and all the blood had been washed down the drain.

She allowed herself to wallow for a couple of days. But eventually, she had to go back to work. The police officer had come round and taken a statement from her. Still, in the end, Laura's death was ruled accidental. Her family were planning the funeral, and Naomi felt sick just thinking about it.

Jake patted her on the shoulder in sympathy when she got to work. "You handle reception today, okay? I'll go and feed the wee beasties." He gave her a thin smile that didn't reach his eyes. At lunchtime, he brought her tea. She let it go cold.

Finally, just as she was getting ready to go home, the front desk phone rang. Jake was already outside, a lit cigarette in his hand. She answered, "Hello? Pawprints cat shelter, how can I help you?"

"Hi," answered a man on the other end of the phone, "I have a stray cat here, a black one. Her collar had your number on it. She looks wet, and I think she has blood on her. Do you want to send someone out to come and get her? I know it's late, but I'd happily keep her at my house overnight and bring her in the morning. Or do you think I should take her to the emergency vet?"

"Sh-She's at your house?" she asked numbly. Her hand began to shake.

"Yes, yes. She came scratching at my door. I live right by a stream, on a public footpath. I think she must have fallen in. She's lucky she didn't drown. Ha! Lucky," the man laughed, "I wonder, is that how she got her name?"

3

A Spectre Calls

Jo A. Ripley

It was a crisp morning that made the ground look like a million diamonds adorned the pavements as the sun's rays glistened all over the ice. These were Sarah's thoughts as she opened her eyes and looked out of her front window. She appreciated the beauty before her, but it was filled with discontent. The street outside had a hauntingly cold and empty feel to it.

She stretched her arms to the ceiling as she rose from her meditation cushion. She wanted to take a moment to enjoy a peek outside at the glorious rays cascading down from the sky. These rays were highlighting the landscape outside, but in the time it had taken her to walk to her window, they had been rudely interrupted by the whimsical behaviour of the very northern unpredictable weather. Suddenly, the sky turned grey, threatening rain.

At this moment, she was overcome with a feeling of apprehension but didn't know why or where it had come from.

Nevertheless, she would not let it bother her, and she gave thanks in her mind for another beautiful day. She took a large breath and exhaled, thanks to the universe. As she let go of her breath, which was supposed to be in a very controlled manner, there was instead a gasp as a book flew off the cabinet and landed on the floor beside her. The pages fluttered and then stopped and fell open on a page with a picture of a huge Raven with the description of the magic that they foretold - in big letters, it said, 'Raven spirit animal brings the gift of prophecy, as shapeshifters they demonstrate the great powers of the spirit world and remind the seer of their immense psychic abilities, should they stop hiding and fully tap into them'. There was an eerie silence, and Sarah could only hear the sound of her own heart beating.

For Sarah, occurrences like this were commonplace but never got any easier to navigate. Aghast, she said aloud, 'What is the message you're trying to give me now?' Life just never felt like it could be straightforward for her, and even though she was a gifted seer, she sometimes wished for a bit of peace in her life. She always wished for some level of normality, but then she knew it was in her blood and not something she could easily get away from, if ever.

She jumped in shock and was startled by a loud "cawwww!!' which shook her to the core, distracted her from looking at the book, and drew her attention outside the window again.

As she looked out of the window, she noticed two huge Ravens swooping down and standing on each of her gate posts at that exact moment. Suddenly, she felt the air evaporate out of her mouth and had no breath. A feeling of dread washed over her body, an ominous feeling that she could not shake.

The peace she had been trying so hard to cultivate had been interrupted as the beady-eyed creatures observed her from afar. They were not taking their eyes off Sarah, and Sarah could not take her eyes off them. Sarah realised she had, in fact, been holding her breath for a good minute. As their eyes appeared to penetrate into her soul, she breathed in slow and shallow as panic gripped her body.

Her first thought was that two people would die today.

It never changed for Sarah when she saw these things. She couldn't stop the panic or the worry of what would happen next. She clutched the window ledge, breathed in, and looked for five things she could see, four things she could touch, and three things she could hear. She stopped at three things she could hear; all she could hear were the bloody birds. She started box breathing, as her psychotherapist had taught her, to ease the stress of living like this. She was aware that people thought she was mad, but she knew she just saw things other people didn't. She had learnt to accept that.

Sarah had been different from others for as long as she could remember.

At the nursery, she would tell people about relatives standing behind them. Apparently, only she could see them.

Or there was that time that she thought it was hilarious when her guardian angel Mark was wearing her dress. Her Mother did not find it funny that she was laughing as the dress, which was on a hanger, swayed side to side while on the back of the door.

Her little brother used to call her 'Matilda', after the smart little character with special powers in her favourite childhood book.

Whatever they thought of her over the years, she had learnt to suppress this ability, but the universe still chose to speak to her in a language it decided she was ready to decipher and interpret.

The Ravens had always been a theme; every time she saw them, she knew death would surely follow and that she needed to prepare.

She recollected the conversation she had days before with her Mother about her Grandmother, who had a dreadful fall and had unfortunately broken her hip. As they sat drinking tea, she warned her Mother that she would not survive the operation and that she should make sure she said her goodbyes. Her Mother had looked shocked and refused to believe what she was hearing. Sarah felt this. She began to doubt herself and tried to convince herself not to worry too much.

But as she saw both Ravens still peering through the window right at her, she knew it was not just one but two people they would lose that day. She suddenly saw a flash of two black hearses. She felt herself reel from the picture inside her mind. After she regained her composure, she told herself not to worry as she replayed the conversation a few days earlier.

As she walked towards the stairs, her phone rang. She picked it up and heard sobbing and crying on the phone. She couldn't make it out at first, but then she heard breaks of sentences between shrieks and cries :

"I think I got here too late…..she was here, and then all of a sudden, as I walked in, she was gone….. they are trying to resuscitate her now".

Sarah raced up the stairs two at a time, the phone in her hand, struggling to grab a pair of trousers and put them on after pulling off her pyjama bottoms in a flurry. She hitched up her trousers with her phone tucked against her shoulder. In order to continue being able to console her Mother and tell her that she was on her way. Suddenly, there were three loud knocks at the door. Sarah ran onto the landing, wondering who it was. Her Mother had heard the knocks too. Sarah wasn't going to bother with changing out of her pyjama top. She ran down the stairs and flung open the front door to be hit by a gust of cold wind, but no sign of anybody.

Not even the Ravens. The street was clear. No one could have run up her steps that fast and made their getaway without her seeing them. Sarah said:

"That's weird, there's no one here!"

Sarah knew immediately what this meant. She felt a shiver run through her spine as another gust of wind hit her, accompanied by the sad realisation that her Grandmother had passed.

Sarah said aloud:

"She's gone".

Sarah's Mother replied:

"Yes, I heard the knocks at the door'.

A second or two later, as Sarah was putting on her coat, she overheard the Nurse break the news that her Grandmother had passed. She felt a deep sadness wash over her heart as she reassured her Mother that she would be there as soon as she could. She felt she had to be the strong one right now. She was always the strong one, being the oldest sibling.

Sarah reminisced about the story of the three knocks, something that her Grandmother had told her happened when a member of the family's soul departed. This was a family story that her Grandma talked about often and something Sarah had never experienced before. She remembered her Grandma when she was a child, telling her ghost stories, taking her on adventures to the local abbey in the car, and turning the headlights off to catch a look at a spectre or two. Looking back, they could have crashed. But nothing stopped a good family ghost hunt on a Friday night; with no parents around, they could do anything. It was so much fun. Being with Grandma was a special world of magic where Sarah could be herself. Grandma told her stories of how her blind Mother could see spirits and tell people who had come to see them from the spirit world when she lost her sight as a child. Everything fascinated Sarah about the peculiar parts of life other people did not see; sometimes, she felt afraid, but mostly, she felt that something was protecting her. She was taught to say her prayers. Be a good girl and not tell lies because God is always watching. Even though God was love, there was karma to pay in life, and we should try to be as helpful as we can to others.

So it was no surprise that the first three knocks should be for Sarah. She was her Grandma's spiritual wing woman. When they were together, they could go to a place where they could talk about secrets no one else talked about. They had various magazines and spooky stories to share and watched unsolved mysteries together. She would miss the way her Grandma twiddled her biscuits between her fingers as she sipped her tea, watching her best programmes. She missed how they made flapjacks together and enjoyed eating them all as they watched the 'scary shows' as Sarah called them.

It was clear to Sarah that Grandma wanted her to know she was okay. Sarah knew she definitely was going to follow the family tradition of knocking on the front door three times when she passed so that she could let her loved ones know that she was okay too. As much as Grandma was fond of the spiritual life, she was afraid of dying and had, over the last few years, started to become upset every time she saw Sarah. She would tell her they could no longer talk about passing because she had become afraid. It was clearly no longer exciting, but now, it was a potential reality that she would soon be a spirit herself. Sarah tried to reassure her, and she said, 'Make sure you let me know whatever happens. You get over safe'. Sarah's mind was transported back to this moment and through her first tears of sadness, there were some tears of joy. A mixture of happiness and sadness came over her like a wave.

As she looked down on the floor, she noticed a written note. On the note was: 'Find the sapphire sword. It was always supposed to be yours.' She knew exactly what this was but did not know how or where to find it. An old family heirloom, a sapphire saracen sword on a brooch that Sarah was shown as a child and was promised to her. It was special because it had been passed down generations. It was Sarah's turn to have it, but sadly, it had gone missing for many years and was mourned by Sarah and her Grandmother. But now that Grandma has passed, is she going to help me find it? she wondered. Sarah had this buoyant feeling that she was being watched over and felt a warm surge of love.

Sarah jumped in the car and met her Mother at the hospital; by this time, the second Raven had slipped her mind. She went in with her sister to hold her Grandma's hand. They took pictures of their hands together. She stroked her Gran's hand and said:

"I'm sorry I wasn't here; I will miss you".

Sarah was sad, but she felt relief. She knew that she was fine. She met with relatives. Her Gran's sister (the only remaining close relative bar the children left), and they shared hugs and kisses. It was a sad day as the Children and Grandchildren lined up to go in. Sarah knew she was still with her, though. She wasn't in her body now but would be there in spirit, watching over them all; she was sure of it.

Sarah got home and made herself a cup of coffee. She needed a breather after a long day at the hospital. She sat and wept for a few minutes. Missing the physical loss of her Grandmother. Following the tears, she fell asleep on the sofa and was woken in darkness by the sound of the phone ringing. Sobbing was heard down the phone:

"He's gone, he's gone!"

A family friend had also passed that very day. A young man suffered a sudden heart attack. No one saw it coming. Two deaths in one day. Sarah gave her condolences. It had definitely been a terrible 24 hours.

That evening, as Sarah was closing her eyes, just drifting off, she felt a hand stroke hers; she said:

"Hello, Grandma".

"I know you have been struggling; why did you tell no one?" Sarah heard.

"I don't like to make a fuss, Gran", replied Sarah in her mind.

"You've been working so hard to raise your girls by yourself, and you deserve some good luck. There's some money on its way for you. In seven days, you will receive a cheque for £7059, and you will be very happy. Do this place up, get yourself something nice, and treat yourself for once," Grandma said.

In the days that passed, the sadness of the loss hit Sarah. She smiled when she thought of the visit she had just had as she was going to sleep. She kept going back to that night - would she have that money? Maybe she was a bit overwhelmed from the passing and imagined it all, she thought to herself.

She spent the coming days working hard and coming home to a cold house, making the kids their tea and trying to make ends meet when she heard a sound.

It was the front door.

There was a brown envelope being pushed through the letterbox.

Sarah opened the letter - a cheque for £7059.

She couldn't believe it.

She thanked her Grandmother out loud and told her she was always welcome to call around anytime she liked.

She picked up the phone to call her Mother, but funnily enough, she noted that her Mother was calling her precisely at the same time. She answered the phone and heard her Mum shout:

"I've got some good news!!" Sarah said:

"So have I, but you go first".

Sarah's Mother had been given a date to move into her new home, and she wanted Sarah to come and take her belongings, which were still there. Sarah told her Mum about her money miracle and how it had been a really strange but good time because she felt looked after from the other side.

Sarah said she would be around later to collect her things and that she did. On entry to the house, she could smell her Grandma's scent." Strange", she thought, but maybe her Mum had the scent to remind her and had been spraying it about. She shouted and went up to her room to collect her things. As she walked up the stairs, her bedroom door creaked open, and Sarah knew there was a presence. She didn't feel afraid and called out:

"Grandma?"

The scent was stronger now. Sarah stood in her room facing outwards when a door creaked open to her Mother's room across the landing of its own accord. Sarah was slow in walking towards them, as she was apprehensive but also intrigued. "Grandma?" she said again.

As she walked in, the scent was apparent, and she heard a whisper:

"On the bed"

Sarah looked inside the room. There were boxes and a few things lying on the bed, ready to be put away. There was a jewellery box with a drawer left open. She noticed the sapphire poking out straightaway. The brooch? How did her

Mother get it? How did it get here? So many questions raced through her mind. It had been missing for so long! Sarah remembered all the conversations when her Grandmother would say it was missing and that she didn't know where it went. She reached her hand out to touch it and pick it up when she heard the door open behind her. Distracted, Sarah turned around to see her Mother in the doorway. Her Mother looked sad and remorseful.

"You, you found it", her voice trembled.

"It was you??" Sarah said.

Her Mother looked ashamed and embarrassed.

"I just wanted it for a little while. I was actually quite sad she never wanted to give it to me. You always seemed so special to her. I wish I had been as special."

At that moment, Sarah could feel anger no longer. She took her Mother in her arms and hugged her. Her Mother wept as she recounted how she was told the brooch would be Sarah's, that she was not to have it, and how disappointed she felt that it would skip being hers. So she took it when no one was looking and kept it. She said she was always going to pass it on but just wanted it for a time.

They agreed that Grandma must have wanted Sarah to have it for her to have found it, so her Mother gave her it there and then. They didn't want angry Grandma knocking about. She was a force to be reckoned with in life, so they laughed, she would probably be much worse in death!

There was relief for both of them because for Sarah, it had been found and was no longer a mystery, and for her Mother, she was able to come clean and have some closure.

When Sarah returned home and took out the brooch, she became overwhelmed with gratitude. Sarah spoke aloud, thanking her Grandma for the unexpected gifts. The idea of her Grandma orchestrating all these blessings from the other side filled Sarah with a sense of wonder. She knew her Grandma, now free from earthly concerns, was still there looking out for her and her family.

With newfound hopes and resources, Sarah followed her Grandma's advice and began planning renovations on her house. She created a warm and inviting space for herself and her girls, transforming the once-cold house into a home filled with love and cherished memories.

As the days turned into weeks, Sarah couldn't help but reflect on the interconnectedness of the spiritual and material worlds. Her bond with her Grandma, now a spiritual wing woman from beyond, seemed stronger than ever. The unexpected financial support served as a reminder that sometimes, even in the midst of her grief, there had been moments of magic and generosity.

Sarah continued honouring her Grandma's memory, sharing stories and lessons with her children. Tales of spirits, unseen connections, and mysterious knocks on the door became part of their family stories. As the years passed, Sarah hoped that one day, when the time came, she and her Grandma would again become spiritual wing women, exploring the realms of mystery and magic together.

4

Peil Island

Dorothy King

Walking down the jetty, I joined the queue for the ferry. A small white boat bobbed on the waves, ploughing towards us. My heart sank. I don't know what I expected, but it was bigger than that. As it nosed into the pier, the ferryman jumped off, landing securely and bringing a mooring rope. Time practiced, and he secured the boat before dropping the ramp so we could board. Three others boarded before I followed, heading towards the prow. Tucking my rucksack between my legs, I gazed over at our destination. A small island with a terrace of eight cottages looked towards the channel; the track in front led up to a large white building. I assumed that was the pub. The Ship Inn, built sometime in the nineteenth century, housed the King of Piel, landlord and overseer of the island. Beyond the pub, a castle stood sentinel watching the south end of Walney Island and the entrance to the channel with its access to the docks.

The jetty on Piel was a lot narrower than at Roa Island. Small leisure craft were tied onto the pier, and anchors were latched into the slats. I was glad that the tide was on the flood so that the walk onto the island was shorter. My first stop was the pub to arrange a site to pitch my tent for a couple of days. That done, tent up, and with a refreshing drink under my belt, I decided to explore

I headed towards the cottages and a track that seemed to stop in the tide. Strange. Some of the cottages were occupied, and the people were friendly and talkative; everyone suggested that I avoid the castle after dark. I wonder why? I carried on along the path, giving fantastic views of Walney Island with its lighthouse and colony of seals on its south end. The castle was just a shadow of its former self. The corner turrets were partly demolished. On a rise, the main body of the buildings stood proud and tall. Shrubs grew up from the floor, and access to the top was barred. As I walked around, I caught movement out of the corner of my eye, but when I turned, there was no one there. Everything seemed familiar, as if I remembered it, but I had never been here before, had I? Old tales of my very distant ancestor living here, a monk no less, drifted into my mind. Shivering, my stomach rumbled, so I headed back for food and a couple of pints before bed. People in the pub were chatty, telling tales of going crabbing, cockling, fishing. On a full moon, they said you would see a monk walking the grounds who drowned in the sands.

'But mind lad, the monks do not like snooping at night.'

'Why?' They shook their heads at my question and talked among themselves. I finished off my beer and headed for bed. Snuggling into my sleeping bag, I was soon asleep.

I don't know what roused me; it was still dark. Pulling on some clothes, I scrambled outside. A full moon illuminated the island, casting interesting shadows. Yachts were moored offshore, gently bobbing. I seemed to be the only one awake. In my head, I replayed the conversations I had with the cottagers. 'What a load of piffle,' I muttered and walked towards the ruins.

At one point, the rising path narrowed dramatically, rocks embedded in the earth lying in wait. Tripping, I threw myself towards the old stone walls; the other way was a steep drop to the rock-strewn beach below. Clutching the wall, I gingerly made my way into the castle bailey. My hands seemed to stick to the stones as a shudder washed over me like water on sand.

Getting my balance seemed easier, so rubbing my hands down the tops of my legs, I gazed around. Moonlight had given way to a daytime cloudy windswept sky. Strange. All the yachts had left. Seeing movement from the corner of my eye, I stepped forward. Amused, I watched a monk with brown hair, sandals, and short-cropped hair. Someone trying to scare me, I guessed. Whoever it was professed not to see me. Walking deeper into the castle, I could see that it seemed complete. The corner turrets are tall, majestic, and entire. Three monks walked out of the central building towards a donkey and cart. Depositing bundles in the back. Determined they would acknowledge me, I positioned myself on their path. All three walked straight through me, not around…through staggering, I reached for a wall to steady myself as another wave of trembling washed over me. A young monk came dashing out of the Keep,

'There you are, Brother Zachariah. We need thy help.'

I started to correct him but decided to play along. Running my hands down my jeans was a nervous habit, and they felt wrong. A course brown fabric like the monk's habit clothed me.

'This is daft; I'm in a dress. How?'

Following, I hoped for answers.

'Take that.' A small barrel was thrust into my arms. 'Hurry, or we will miss the tide.'

Depositing our burdens, the wagon was full. Over full to my mind. 'You guide Jobe.' The monk instructed me as he clambered aboard. I complied, wondering how long this charade would continue. The donkey, Jobe, strained to start the cart moving. Head down, he plodded on. Through the arched gateway, over the mote bridge, down the east side of the island, where were the cottages? We descended onto the beach. The poor animal seemed exhausted, head down, breathing strained; we plodded across the sands. Water was running in the first gutter, but Jobe trudged down the incline gamely. He stumbled, knocking me backwards. The wagon tipped, throwing the poor animal over, breaking its neck, and trapping my legs and hips. I couldn't move. Trying to unload the cart, the monk dislodged its load, and its contents cascaded over me, holding me down. The tide was on the flood.

We will pray for you, Brother Zachariah.' With that, he turned and ran for his life. Saltwater lapped around my head, filling my ears, stinging my eyes, covering my face…

Spluttering, I woke up, my heart pounding, my head out of the tent, and my face in the drizzle that enveloped Piel. Wriggling backwards, I squirmed out of my sleeping bag. Sand spilt over the ground sheet. I reached for my clothes. Sun peeped through the clouds, warming the day. Changing into my shorts, I noticed a rough brown rag in a crumpled heap in my tent. A torn, wet habit. Gosh, I was stiff. I tried to rub a mark on my leg. It was a bruise; I was covered in them, my legs, hips, and torso. It was as if I had been pummeled...

5

The Unwelcome Guest

Pamela Edwards

Eva never expected anything extraordinary to happen on what seemed like a perfectly ordinary day. It was the mid-80s, and her life was a routine blend of work, family, and the occasional evening out. That morning, she had dropped the kids off at school, as usual, and headed to her office at the self-drive hire company she ran with her brother. The day was supposed to be just like any other—dealing with accounts, customer inquiries, and general administrative work. But fate had other plans.

As Eva arrived at the office, she was greeted by the mechanic, a burly man named Dave, who usually had a calm demeanour. Today, however, his face was ashen, and his eyes were wide with something Eva could only describe as fear. Her first thought was that there had been an accident with one of the vehicles, but as she stepped out of her car, she noticed something unusual—stones were being hurled across the yard. It wasn't just a few pebbles; it was as if someone was launching a full-scale attack.

"Who's doing this?" Eva asked, ducking as another stone whizzed past her head.

"That's the thing," Dave said, his voice trembling. "There's no one out there. It's just... happening."

Eva's scepticism kicked in. She'd never been one for ghost stories or the supernatural, and she was sure there had to be a logical explanation. Maybe some kids were playing a prank, hiding somewhere out of sight. But as the morning wore on, it became clear that this was no ordinary prank. Every time anyone stepped out of the office, they were pelted with stones. Some of the stones were small, but others were large enough to leave a mark. Even inside the office, Eva could hear the stones rolling across the roof of the newly purchased Porta-Cabin.

The situation escalated when Eva, alone in her office, was searching through the phone book for the number of the local church. On the wall opposite her desk sat a small filing cabinet with various items on top, including a baby's shoe that had been left behind in one of the vehicles. As Eva flipped through the pages, she saw something that made her heart stop—the baby's shoe lifted off the cabinet, hovered for a moment, and then, with a force that was impossible to ignore, flew across the room, hitting her square in the chest. The impact left a bruise, not just on her skin but on her psyche.

Eva let out a scream so loud that Dave came running from the workshop. She bolted out of the office, her breath coming in short, panicked gasps. She knew this wasn't a simple prank. Something far more sinister was at play.

"What the hell was that?" Dave asked, his eyes darting around the office as if expecting the shoe to fly back at them.

"I don't know," Eva whispered, her voice shaking. "But I'm starting to think we're not alone here."

The day only grew stranger. Papers flew off shelves, heavy folders crashed onto Eva's desk, and a sense of unease settled over the office. When Eva finally managed to contact the local priest, she was met with bureaucratic hurdles—he needed permission from the Bishop before he could investigate, and the Bishop was away for weeks. In the meantime, Eva and Dave were left to face whatever was haunting them.

Days turned into weeks, and the strange occurrences continued. Stones kept flying, objects moved on their own, and a sense of dread hung over the office. Eva found herself unable to go to work, crippled by panic attacks every time she got close to the site. She spoke to a friend, someone with a deep interest in spirituality, who suggested wrapping herself in a "protection bubble" and trying to communicate with the spirit. Desperate to keep her job and regain some semblance of normalcy, Eva decided to try it.

One morning, armed with her invisible protection, Eva walked into the office and, when she was alone, spoke aloud. "Fred," she said, using the name she and Dave had given to their unseen tormentor, "I just want to do my work. I won't bother you if you don't bother me. Can we make a deal?"

From that moment on, things seemed to calm down—for Eva, at least. The stones stopped flying when she was in the yard, and the objects in her office stayed in place. But for the others, especially the younger mechanics who enjoyed provoking the spirit with loud music, the hauntings grew more intense. One young mechanic even ended up with clear bite marks on his arm, much to everyone's horror.

As the summer wore on, Eva's brother decided to call in a professional—a local medium with a reputation for dealing with stubborn spirits. The medium confirmed their worst fears: the spirit haunting their office was that of a medieval soldier, disturbed from his rest when the Porta-Cabin had been stationed at a castle during renovations. The soldier was angry, feeding off the energy of the young mechanic, and had no intention of leaving.

Despite the medium's efforts to guide the spirit into the light, the soldier refused to pass over. The medium warned that the spirit's energy would eventually dissipate, but it would take time. In the meantime, Eva and her team would have to learn to live with their ghostly guest.

The story of the haunted office quickly spread through the town, attracting unwanted attention from both the press and paranormal investigators. One professor from Nottingham University even spent a week at the site, documenting the strange occurrences. Eva herself had a terrifying encounter when she felt the spirit pass right through her, leaving her frozen in place as the professor's equipment spiked with energy readings.

Eventually, the activity did begin to fade, just as the medium had predicted. The company moved into a new, purpose-built office, and the haunting became a distant memory—until one day, Fred returned.

It happened on an ordinary afternoon. Eva went down to the workshop to check on a truck that had been locked up overnight. The mechanics were frustrated; the key wouldn't turn in the lock. Jokingly, Eva mentioned Fred, and the mechanics, who hadn't been told of the haunting, turned pale. Eva spoke to Fred aloud, asking him to unlock the door. To everyone's astonishment, the door clicked open. The mechanics were terrified, but Eva simply thanked Fred and went back to her office, a small smile on her lips.

Fred's visits became infrequent, but each time he returned, Eva knew how to handle him. Over time, the spirit's presence faded completely, leaving Eva with a story she rarely told. But every now and then, when she found herself alone in a quiet room, she would think of Fred and the strange summer that changed her life forever.

Eva wasn't sure if anyone would believe her story, but she knew it was true. And in the years that followed, as she delved deeper into spirituality and developed her intuition, she realized that Fred had been the beginning of a journey— one that would lead her to many more "spooky" moments and a deeper understanding of the world beyond the veil.

6

The House That Wasn't There

Margaret Martindale

Margaret felt old—so very old—as she huddled in the worn armchair, her body shivering despite the warmth of the fire burning low in the hearth. The chill that had settled into her bones went unnoticed, just as the rapidly fading light outside the window did. Her mind was elsewhere, drifting back to a time when she was young, when life was full of promise and the future stretched endlessly before her.

The memories wrapped around her like a familiar blanket, more vivid now than the dim room around her. She smiled faintly as she thought about the whirlwind of years spent building a home and raising her two daughters. Amber, her eldest, had always been a grounded child, deeply connected to nature. She became a hedge witch, concocting potions from herbs she gathered in the woods, a true country girl who still checked in on her old mother regularly.

But Jade, her younger daughter, had been different. Jade had been a daddy's girl, with a love for cars and a thirst for adventure that had taken her far from home. Since Ben, Margaret's husband, had passed, Jade's visits and calls had become rare. Margaret understood—Jade had her own life now, a life that didn't include the quiet rhythms of the countryside where Margaret remained.

Margaret's thoughts turned to Ben, the man who had stolen her heart so many years ago. He had been a dashing young man, full of kindness and patience. Margaret hadn't been looking for love when they met; she was still reeling from the wreckage of a past relationship, but Ben's persistence won her over. What she had wanted was a friend—what she got was the love of her life.

Those early days with Ben were some of the happiest Margaret had ever known. They travelled all over the country in old, unreliable cars, laughing as they broke down in the middle of nowhere. Jade, ever her father's shadow, would help him fix the engine while Amber wandered off to gather plants, her nose always buried in some new book on herbal remedies. The memories of those carefree days brought a smile to Margaret's face.

But, as children do, Amber and Jade grew up and forged their own paths. Amber married young, and Margaret remembered making her wedding dress—simple and elegant, just like her daughter. Not long after, their granddaughter Laura was born, and as grandparents, Ben and Margaret spoiled her every chance they got.

Jade, however, followed a different road, working odd jobs to fund her travels around the world. She eventually settled in South Africa, much to Ben and Margaret's worry. It wasn't the safest place, but Jade thrived there. She married and started her own business, and the last Margaret heard, Jade was doing well.

A sudden chill brought Margaret back to the present. The fire had burned low, and she realized it was time for bed. Her joints protested as she rose from the chair, but she managed to climb the stairs and crawl under the covers, pulling the blankets tight around her. As she drifted off to sleep, her mind wandered again, this time back to her childhood, to the memories of her sisters. She hadn't been close to most of them, except for the youngest.

She remembered the night her youngest sister was born—the rush to find her father, the first cries of the baby, and her mother being ill afterward. Margaret had taken on the responsibilities of feeding the baby, changing nappies, and pushing her pram through the village. As the memories played out in her mind, they shifted once more, to her sister's wedding day. Amber and Jade had been flower girls, scattering rose petals as the newlyweds emerged from the church.

But then, as dreams often do, her thoughts took an unexpected turn. Margaret found herself back in the days of her courtship with Ben. They would meet in the evenings after work, sometimes late, depending on her shifts. They would find a quiet pub for a drink, then drive through the dark, winding lanes, hoping to find a secluded spot where they could be alone.

One night, they had stopped at a gateway near an old castle. It looked like it might have once been a lane, but a farmer had blocked it off with a gate. The trees lining the track were bare, their skeletal branches reaching out like bony fingers under the near-full moon. Everything was bathed in an eerie black-and-grey light.

They were just settling in for a cuddle when Margaret noticed something at the top of the hill—four distinct rectangles of light, like windows glowing in the darkness. A sudden chill ran through her, and she began to shiver uncontrollably. Fear gripped her, an inexplicable terror that made her want to flee.

"What are those lights at the top of the hill?" she asked, her voice trembling.

Ben glanced at the hill, then back at her. "It's just the moon," he said.

"No, those lights in the windows," she insisted, pointing toward the hill.

Ben looked again, but his expression didn't change. "I don't see any lights. There's nothing up there, just a field."

But Margaret couldn't shake the feeling of dread. "Please, take me home. I can't stay here. It's too scary."

Ben chuckled softly, but he saw the seriousness in her eyes and didn't argue. He started the car and drove her home. They never returned to that spot, though they passed it many times on the way to visit Ben's parents. Margaret had tried to forget about those strange lights, but the memory lingered, a shadow in the back of her mind.

Years passed, and Margaret never mentioned the lights again, not even to Ben. Life was too busy, and the memory faded, buried under the weight of years. But now, as she lay in bed, the memory resurfaced with startling clarity. The fire had long since gone out, and the room was icy cold, but Margaret felt something else—a presence, a sensation she hadn't felt in decades.

Suddenly, she was back at that lonely track, the moon's light painting the branches black, just like before. The same fear gripped her heart, squeezing it tight. She could see the lights again, those four glowing rectangles at the top of the hill. Only this time, they weren't distant—they were coming closer, moving down the hill toward her.

Margaret's breath caught in her throat. She tried to move, to reach for the lamp by her bedside, but her body wouldn't respond. She was frozen in place, her eyes locked on the advancing lights. They were almost at the gate now, the glow so intense it lit up the entire room.

Then, just as suddenly as they had appeared, the lights blinked out, leaving Margaret in total darkness. For a moment, she thought it was over, that whatever it was had gone. But then she felt it—a hand, cold and skeletal, gripping her arm.

Margaret gasped, her heart pounding in her chest as she tried to pull away, but the hand held fast. The darkness around her seemed to pulse, and she realised with a growing horror that she wasn't alone.

The presence loomed over her, and she could feel its breath, icy and malevolent, on her face. Panic surged through her, and she opened her mouth to scream, but no sound came out.

And then, in a voice that seemed to echo from the depths of her own mind, she heard it whisper, "You shouldn't have come back."

The lights flared again, blinding her, and in that instant, Margaret knew the truth—those lights, that presence, had been waiting for her all these years. Waiting for her to return to that place where she had once glimpsed the unknown.

But this time, there was no escape.

As the light consumed her, Margaret's last thought was of Ben, and how she wished she could tell him that she finally understood. The past was never truly gone—it was always there, waiting to reclaim those who tried to forget.

The house was silent, the only sound the soft ticking of the clock on the mantelpiece. The next morning, when the nurse arrived to find the bed empty and cold, she knew before she even checked that Margaret had gone. All that remained was the faint smell of something burned, and on the pillow, a single silver hair, glowing faintly in the morning light.

7

A Raven Freed: A story of two worlds

Laura Billingham

We hate you!"

"Witch."

"Ugly cow."

"Spooky bitch."

Raven stood among the circle of jeering girls – her classmates – and felt tears welling in her deep brown eyes.

Every day was the same.

Every day, she had to navigate the taunts, the name-calling, the finger-pointing…and sometimes, like today, the punches, pinches and shoves.

ENOUGH!

Bursting through the circle, she ran full tilt into the woods bordering the school playing fields. Running blindly, oblivious to the brambles that tried to trip her and the low-growing branches that appeared to grab her clothing, she pushed on… deeper and deeper into the wood.

Behind, she could hear the shrieks of the other girls as they attempted to pursue her.

"Get her!"

"I'm gonna hurt her this time!"

"Bloody bitch knocked me over, gonna do the same to her when I catch her."

A terrified sob caught in Raven's throat; it sounded as though they were gaining on her. Her breathing was laboured and ragged; she was running out of strength – and options; she had to stop and think for a moment.

Coming to a halt by a beautiful old oak tree, she rested her head on its gnarly trunk and mentally sent a fervent prayer for help out to the Universe. The girls were definitely closer now; Raven could only hope she would be out of sight behind the enormous tree.

The old oak was on the periphery of a small round clearing, where nothing but grass and a few tiny white flowers seemed to flourish. "Weird", Raven thought to herself. The clearing even seemed to have a different light to it from the rest of the woodland. A pale golden haze hung in the air above the circular space.

The oak seemed to be giving her his strength, and she thanked the tree for his support. Her breath was coming slightly easier now; she would be able to run some more – if she had to.

Then she heard…

"I see the bitch!"

With no conscious thought other than to escape, Raven headed directly towards the clearing, it was as though it was calling her. Behind her, the noise of several teenage girls running disturbed the peace of the woodland. Raven ran, fleet of foot once more, and entered the clearing.

"Where the hell did she go?!" was the last thing she heard.

Panting, Raven stood in the centre of the clearing, her pursuers nowhere in sight. Taking a full 360 look around and listening hard, she could neither see nor hear the girls. Whatever had just happened to her (or her tormenters), she was grateful for the respite and sank gratefully to the ground.

The soft green grass welcomed her, and she lay on her back, looking up at a clear blue sky, breathing in the scents of the woodland around her and the grass below her. It had been a long time since she had felt so at peace; in fact, she couldn't remember when she felt so calm and at peace with her surroundings.

For the first time in her life, Raven felt safe. She closed her eyes and let the peace wash over her. The only sounds of nature were the soft susurration of leaves being stirred by a gentle breeze, the happy chittering of birds, and the hum of bees and insects. With a contented sigh, she lowered her eyelids and drifted off into a deep, restful sleep.

The sun was still high in the sky when she awoke some time later, feeling incredibly rested and curiously energised. Coming to a seated position, she surveyed the space around her; everything looked the same as when she had run into the clearing to escape her pursuers…and yet, somehow, it was different.

She was different too. Her drab grey school uniform had transformed into something silky in emerald green, shot through with threads of bright, glittering gold. "I'm dreaming," she said out loud, "I must be."

"You're not dreaming." A hundred quiet voices contradicted her.

Startled, Raven jumped to her feet, the dress flowing and melding softly to her lithe body. Her long dark hair, usually contained in a tight ponytail, now cascaded down her back in glorious waves. At first, she couldn't see anyone, but suddenly, she began to notice female forms in the trees.

"She sees us now," a silvern voice giggled. May we go and greet her?"

"You may my dears, but please do not frighten her."

To Raven's astonishment, the female forms she had spotted began to peel away from the trees and head towards her in a sea of shimmering green, gold and russet. Soon, she was surrounded by a multitude of beautiful creatures – all talking at once.

After her experience with her persecutors, this was all too much for Raven, and she sank to her knees, hands over her ears. And yet she wasn't afraid, far from it; in fact, it was only the noise of the myriad different voices all welcoming her and asking questions that overwhelmed her senses.

"Sssssh," the other, calmer, deeper voice interjected, "what did I say about not frightening the child?"

The lighter voices stopped chattering immediately, and Raven raised her head.

"Who are you? What's happening to me?" To her own ears, she sounded rather timid, so she added in a more forceful tone... "and why am I here?"

The crowd of gorgeous creatures directly in front of her parted, creating a corridor through which strode the most beautiful and statuesque woman Raven had ever seen. There was a presence about the woman that spoke of nature, eternity, strength, and infinite possibilities. Raven was instantly comforted, and she rose to stand before the woman, head bowed in respect.

"I will answer all of these questions and more Raven, but first, let me take you to my home. I'm sure it has been a strange day for you, and you need to eat, drink, and find your balance."

She extended a slender yet muscular arm adorned with golden bracelets that jingled and clinked together in an almost musical fashion, and Raven took hold of the proffered hand. Together, they walked silently out of the sunlit clearing and into a part of the woodland Raven had never visited before. The other creatures seemed to fade quietly away.

"You will see them again soon," the woman said as if sensing Raven's thoughts.

After a short walk through trees that appeared to bow gently as they passed, Raven was led through a door in the trunk of the most enormous tree she had ever seen. Her amazement grew even further when the doorway opened into a space so large it could not possibly have fitted into the circumference of even that huge tree.

She gasped, and the woman laughed, a glorious, rich sound full of joy and appreciation. "Yes, it is, as the Doctor in your favourite TV programme says...bigger on the inside. You will, my dear, find that all things are possible if only you believe. Now come."

She indicated a side room and followed Raven into what appeared to be an empty space. With a wave of her hand, a table appeared. It was laden with fruit and dishes of food with such delicious aromas that Raven's mouth immediately began to water.

"Sit, eat, drink, and when you have had your fill, we will talk."

Raven sat on the chair indicated by the older woman. It was beautifully carved with intricate images of acorns and oak leaves, and despite the lack of padding or cushion, it was the most comfortable chair she had ever sat upon.

"That is because it was created just for you." Her companion said as if reading her mind.

Inexplicably, this sounded perfectly normal to Raven. Why shouldn't a chair have been created for her? She had always had an affinity for oak trees, she even wore a silver acorn and oak leaf on a slender chain around her neck.

The food was divine. She ate her fill and then some more, and with every mouthful she took, the strange situation she was in began to feel more and more comfortable – as if she was always meant to have been there.

With a final satisfied sigh, Raven put down her fork, took a mouthful of water from a crystal goblet, and sat back in her chair.

"All done?" The woman asked.

"Yes, for now." Raven grinned and rubbed her full stomach.

The Woodland Queen, for that was how Raven was beginning to perceive the older woman, laughed heartily and replied, "That is the magic in this place starting to work on you. Now, I am going to tell you a story that will answer all of your questions. Come with me."

The two women, one small, slender and dark of hair, the other more voluptuous with hair the colour of Autumn leaves shot through with gold, moved into a small, cosy chamber. Raven deposited herself on an inviting pile of soft cushions whilst the Woodland Queen reclined in a sculptural wooden chair that appeared to be growing out of the very walls of the room.

"Are you sitting comfortably?" Raven nodded. "Then I'll begin," said the Queen in an obvious parody of a very old-school British radio presenter.

Raven listened with rapt attention to a story so strange it had to be true.

When she had run away from her classmates (was that only this morning, she wondered to herself), she had inadvertently stumbled into the portal that separated the human world from the Faerie realm. The clearing she had happened upon was normally only visible at specific times of the year; ordinarily, the space looked just like any other part of the woodland, which explained why she hadn't recognised the spot despite spending so much time in amongst the trees.

Her fervent prayer to the Universe while sheltering by the oldest oak tree in the wood had activated the portal, and she had passed through to a world where magik ruled and humans didn't exist.

"But…" Raven began to interrupt at this point to say she was a human. The Queen merely raised one eyebrow and continued to speak.

"Did you ever feel at home in the human realm? Did you ever have any friends or know your family?"

"Well…no…I was found as a newborn baby in a forest, underneath an oak tree apparently, and spent most of my childhood in foster care and children's homes. I was called *different,* and no one wanted to adopt me."

"You ARE different, Raven, and so very special...listen..."

The Queen told Raven of a time long ago when many of humankind could cross to the Faeries realm. A time when the veils separating the two worlds were paper thin and easily breached. Humans and those in the faery realm didn't fear each other, and both worlds lived in harmony with nature. But when mankind began to move away from the rhythms of nature, the world of man became separated from that of the Fae.

At the same time, perhaps infected by the human world, some of the Fae began to question the rule of the Woodland Queens – an ancient and proud line which had passed from mother to daughter from the beginning of time. An ancient legend, even in Fae terms, foretold the divisions between humans and Fae and within the Fae themselves, and of the girl child who would mend the rifts. The Queen and her entourage had retreated to the oldest forests to await the arrival of the one named in the old legend as Raven.

Raven gasped at the mention of her name.

Time passed until the day the Queen, alone in her forest realm, encountered a human man who had somehow crossed the barrier. By some miracle, her people, who were able to merge with the trees in the forests and bore the name Dryads, had not spotted his arrival, and thus, it was left to the Queen to address his confusion.

Unlike most of the other humans she occasionally sent her ravens to spy upon to ascertain what was happening in the world of men, he was in tune with nature and was loving, kind, and intelligent. The Queen, devoid of male companionship and longing for an heir to inherit her mantle, shared his makeshift bed, and his child grew inside her—a child of neither realm and yet of both.

When the baby was born, the man wished to take her to his world to meet his family, but the Queen forbade it…knowing as she did that many years would have passed in his world during the time he had dwelt in hers. But he didn't listen, and in the dead of night whilst the Queen slept, he stole the child away and, with the help of a few Dryads who had become jealous of the Queen's love for him, he was able to cross back to the human world.

But the man was not prepared for what had confronted him – nearly 1500 years had elapsed since he had passed through the portal. His family was long gone, and the human world had changed beyond all recognition. Where once had been woodland, now there were shiny pathways lined with box-like houses – quite unlike the round dwellings of his old village. Great metal beasts charged down the shiny paths, belching fumes that tickled his nose and made him cough, and in the air, he spied giant metal birds.

Terrified, he ran back to the clearing in the wood, only to find it was no longer there. In a panic, he placed his baby daughter at the base of a great old oak tree and ran deeper into the woodland, shouting for his Queen. He was still shouting for her when he ran out of the woodland onto a busy road and into the path of an articulated lorry.

Later that same day, a walker out with his dog stumbled across a baby girl – a raven was watching over her, or so the man said – and so the foundling child was given the name – Raven.

The bearer of this name smiled; she had been told the story of her discovery many times but hadn't believed it.

The Queen had no way to rescue her baby girl, but she knew the child would come looking for her when the time was right – even if she wasn't aware that's what she was doing.

"When you sent out your prayer for help to the Universe, the trees heard you, in particular the great old oak, and they sent a message to the world of the Fae that you were in the woods and needed my help. I was able to open the portal – and here you are."

"You're my mother?" Raven asked the question, but in her heart, she already knew the answer.

"Yes, you are my daughter and will one day wear this crown." The Queen smiled and touched the small golden diadem of interlinked leaves that rested on her head.

Raven was stunned, it all sounded so bizarre, odd, and fanciful. And yet…and yet…she knew it to be true. Every atom in her body resonated with this woman, her mother, and with everything in this realm. A feeling of belonging filled her with joy – she was finally where she was meant to be. There was nothing and no one in the human world she would miss. All her life, she had been the outcast, the outsider, the girl with no roots, no family – and here she was, finally home – and in some strange and twisted way, it was down to those schoolgirl bullies.

"How long has it been for you?" She asked her mother.

"Not long – perhaps two hours as you used to measure time."

"But I'm seventeen!"

"And yet you are still my newborn child, my love – with so much to learn. Now you are here, I can begin to remind you what you already know – the memories you carry will resurface now you are back in your rightful place."

Raven approached the beautiful woman she now knew to be her mother and was enveloped in her embrace – it felt so right.

As the two women sat side by side, the Queen told Raven of the ancient legend and the part she would play in it. Raven, the daughter of a Fae Queen and a human man, was to become the bridge between the two worlds. In the timeline Raven had just left, many humans were questioning how they lived and seeking out the old ways, the old magik. By the time Raven would be crowned Queen herself, humanity should have undergone a radical change of direction and the way would be open for Fae and humanity to live in unity once more.

"That time is not yet," the Queen stressed, seeing the panic on Raven's face. "My dear, you have many Fae years to learn and grow. I will not succumb to death and resurrection until you are ready to take on my mantle – on that you can be assured. But you are the girl the legend tells of, and you will be the one to reunite the realms…when the time is right."

Raven relaxed. For the first time in her life, she knew who she was, and she could see a future—a future where she would make a difference. It was empowering, exhilarating, and exciting even. She had a mother who would help her grow and learn. There would be no more running from the bullies, no more living every day feeling lost, scared, and alone.

She was Raven.

She was of both worlds.

She was the bridge.

She was the future.

8

The Raven Geomancer

Ellie LaCrosse

The wind skimmed the stones, standing proudly in orderly circles. This was an ancient site before man recorded history but told stories. The small monoliths had listened to so many yarns, had eavesdropped secrets and collected the energy trapped in blood and sweat over millennia.

Locals called them 'Dancing Stones'. Legends abounded of sacred dances, energy drawn and dispersed at different times of the year. The true nature of creating the circles during the Bronze Age had long been forgotten. It didn't mean it wasn't real; the supernatural giants turned to stone, a race memory and networks of earth forces now burned out by modernity.

The views over the peninsula were sweeping, and on a clear day, the rope-like curve of the bay was visible spanning many miles even as the crow flew. Only local people visited or dedicated diviners searched out archaic landscape engineering, the fragments of original patterns remembered in nature. The local dowsing society would meet by the stones to try and trace primeval Ley lines, demarcating prehistoric tracks.

Often mocked by farmers who saw them as a nuisance trampling over their pastures with their copper rods or pendulums. However, the local group managed to plot out features and tracks that all radiated from the concentric stone circles.

When touching the stones, a flutter or tingling sensation was still possible, especially if the person was still and allowed the sensation to build up. For weird reasons, wildlife was attracted to or repelled by the site. Birds generally seemed attracted.

An unkindness of ravens often gathered near the stone site. Observers noted their odd ritual 'dances' atop the stone shapes, bowing, cawing, swopping and weaving up and down the circles. There were often battles between the seagulls trying to steal picnic offerings from visitors. The ravens often won with greater agility; their beaks and claws were more suited to combat and inflict damage.

The stones appeared to glow when the sun set, especially during mid-summer, with the quartz glistening in the strong sunshine. The furry coating of lichen clinging on in patches softened the feel. The pathways down to the coastline spread out trampled gaps between the gorse, scrub, and barren rocky crags nearby. Sheep nestled near the stones during scouring winter squalls and nibbled the softer grass that grew at the stones' base.

One fine day, when the scene was benign, and the sea shimmered on the horizon, a young woman flopped down by the stones and spread out a tartan rug to sit on. She was quite young, maybe a teenager. She adjusted her floral headband, which was exactly the pattern that matched her summer dress, swept her long auburn hair off her face, grabbed a pair of sunglasses to keep the sun from her eyes, and started to read a book. After some time, she looked at her watch as if waiting for someone to visit her. Then, she reached into the picnic basket she'd brought along. She produced a bottle of wine and took a swig, wiping her mouth with her hand, leaving a faint crimson stain on the back.

Sometime later, a lone raven startled the girl by settling onto the stone nearest to where she was sitting. It started 'chattering', which unnerved her. She almost thought she could hear voices or conversation, which was odd as the site lacked visitors. Even the sheep were gathered some distance away.

Worryingly for the girl, more ravens came and sat individually atop each stone until she was surrounded. It was mysterious and sent a chill up the girl's spine. She flapped her arms away imperiously towards the ravens. They suddenly lifted off together, creating drama, but they kept circling around high in the sky above the stones.

The air crackled with electricity, it was sizzling hot. The girl started to sigh and looked anxiously around her like she was expecting someone to join her. She grabbed the bottle of wine again and took a larger gulp. Shortly afterwards, the warmth from the stones lulled her to slumber, and she slumped against one of the stones.

During her dream, she felt very 'light'. It felt delicious and comforting, as though she was drifting through the air with the ravens, spiralling up across the peninsula. As she fluttered her eyelids to awaken, she felt trapped in a lucid dream. She was still floating above the stone circle. She shouted out, but no sound came from her mouth. With mounting unease, she viewed the landscape shape-shift, and an emotion of clairvoyance swept over her as the scene below her was revealed.

As she was 'watching', she 'saw' her boyfriend approaching the stone circle and talking to what looked like another girl waiting on the tartan rug. Was it her? She was wearing the same clothes and hairband, but she was struggling to view her face. She still couldn't tell if it was her. It was unnerving. The boyfriend gave an excuse for being late and offered more bread and wine he'd been carrying. She watched the pair entwine and share a lover's embrace, but something seemed amiss; she drew a sharp intake of breath when she realised it was herself she had been 'viewing'.

She shouted out, but again, silence and no sound escaped. She attempted to move but was pinned by an invisible energy surrounding her. It was almost like she was stuck in a clear perspex tube high above the stones with circling ravens, her constant companions.

Quickly, the scene changed to something more dangerous and dark. The boyfriend ripped the dress in his ardour, and the young woman screamed and pushed him off her. This appeared to enrage him, and he roughly agitated her so hard she tried to escape his clutches. She stumbled, fell and smacked her head against a standing stone. A vivid pool of blood spread underneath her head, a stain of bright red smeared across one edge of an upright stone.

The boyfriend stared silently for a long time in a panic. He put his hand to his mouth as if to suppress a scream, then grabbed the woman's legs and dragged her several yards to a crevice in the limestone crag nearby to try to hide the body, then ran back to his car.

She felt a flutter of raven wing swoosh past her face. The raven geomancer spell was broken, and the young woman blinked awake.

She stretched out, yawned, and thought she'd had a strange and unsettling dream. She felt like she'd consumed too much wine. She checked her watch again, impatiently reached into her bag for her phone, and called her boyfriend.

"Where are you, hun? I've been up here on my lonesome for ages and started the wine!"

"Sweetheart, I'm just running late. I'm off now for the rest of the afternoon. Would you like me to pop to the Co-op on the way and pick up more wine and bread?"

"I'm already a bit squiffy. Oh, go on then. Will you be okay driving? Shall we order a taxi and pick the car up tomorrow?"

"See what happens, eh? See you shortly."

While she spent yet more time away waiting for her lover, the ravens paid her a return visit, so she started throwing crust crumbs at them. She regretted it as a mob descended and sat on the stones, waiting for their free snacks.

Curiously, the ravens started chattering again, flew individually, and sat on a stone. They all began to turn around in synchronicity. The young woman was mesmerised as she watched the strange display. Suddenly, the warm stone she was propped up against became cold and started slipping. With a start, she realised she was 'stuck' to the surface of the stone, and it gathered energy by rotating slowly at first. Her hair started to stand on end; her necklace levitated from her neck until it was perpendicular to her body.

All the stones with the ravens sitting on them started to rotate, gathering speed. The energy released crackled in the air. The landscape again shaped-shifted and blurred into streaks of green, blue and white. A pain started to throb in her head, and she felt nauseous.

The landscape had changed, but she could still make out the outline of the peninsula and the location of the stone circles. The pain quickly subsided, and she felt incredibly weightless again. An upward force was pushing higher and higher off the ground, spinning into a vortex. Unlike the pleasant sensation she experienced last time, the pressure on her felt like wading through a forcefield. Although she was light, the air felt thick and charged. She tried to scream again, but no sound was emitted, terrified she'd be dashed to her death below, so high was the force spinning her.

The raven mob flew in and out of the vortex, swirling ever higher, cawing and mimicking human voices, "Blood toucheth blood! Blood toucheth blood!" They were circling her. It was almost like they were protecting her, but the terror increased when she scanned the white stones, and the words, 'Blood toucheth blood' chillingly appeared over the stones in fresh, dripping blood. She saw the scene in real-time in a blink as her boyfriend arrived at the stones below and searched for her. She observed him striding over to the rug and scratching his head.

She frantically tried to attract his attention, to move her arms, but she was pinned against this invisible swirling prison above the stones. He looked around the site frantically, searching around the concentric stones, growing more and more frustrated and impatient. She observed him looking at his phone watch. She overheard him calling her.

"Where are you? I thought you were waiting here. Are you playing games because you're brassed off?"

He then threw the bag with the purchased wine and bread in a huff and strode back to his car. The young woman then had a deja-vu moment, and horror struck her when she recognised her face from her lucid dream. She let out blood-curdling screams, and this time, the sound pierced the forcefield. She came around propped up against a large white stone in the middle of the stone circle facing the sea.

Had she witnessed her death?

Reassuringly, she scanned the stones nearby and couldn't see traces of blood anywhere, but the tartan rug and picnic hamper had vanished. Frightened, she left the location and started running to the nearby road. It felt like a premonition to her, and she had to flee—she had to escape this unfathomable situation.

She scrambled through the trampled sheep paths and was directed by a solitary raven, almost showing her the ancient route that led down to a rocky limestone ridge. She spotted a shortcut to the road over the ridge. The lone raven swooped down nearby on the highest jut of rock, stopped, and tapped its beak on the rock edge. Fascinated, she watched for a few seconds as if the raven was trying to show her something.

She spotted a blood trail as she peered over the edge of the limestone crevice. Her heart froze. Some way down into the abyss of the fractured limestone pavement, there was a blood-soaked hairband!

The last memory before she fainted and tumbled down the ravine was the raven cawing, "Blood toucheth blood!"

9

Death's Door

Margaret Martindale

Suddenly, I jolted awake.

"Where am I?" The question echoed in my mind, heavy with confusion. This isn't my bed—I'm sure of it. Everything feels wrong: the mattress is too big, too soft, too foreign. I reach for some semblance of familiarity, but my thoughts slip away like sand through my fingers. Who am I? My own name dances on the edge of my consciousness, just out of reach.

I glance around the room, trying to ground myself in my surroundings. A dress hangs in front of me, and my eyes fixate on it, trying to make sense of what I'm seeing. It's hideous, a tattered thing that looks as if it's been woven from cobwebs and dirtied with dark, crimson stains. My stomach churns. The room is otherwise bare, save for the bed I'm lying in.

Two doors stand on the wall opposite me, their presence both ominous and intriguing. From behind one, I hear the distant murmur of voices. The words are muffled, indistinct, but something deep inside me knows they hold importance. I strain to listen, but as I do, the other door flies open with a loud bang.

"She's awake!" someone shouts, the voice too loud, too harsh.

I shrink back, pulling the covers over my head as if they could shield me from the noise. The sound reverberates through my skull, too intense to process. I need silence— space to understand what's happening. But the person doesn't stop. They dance around the bed, their chatter relentless, grating against my frayed nerves. Slowly, mercifully, the noise begins to fade, and I slip back into unconsciousness.

The next time I wake, it's like emerging from a dense fog. Everything around me is blurred, indistinct, as if I'm seeing it through a veil. Gradually, the room comes into focus: the same oversized bed, the same drab walls, the same awful dress hanging like a spectre in the corner.

A new presence enters the room, quiet and gentle. Was she here before? I can't remember. She speaks softly, asking if I'd like to get up. Her voice is soothing, a balm to my frazzled senses. I turn to look at her, to thank her—and then I see her face. It's just a skull.

A scream rips from my throat, and the world collapses into darkness.

When I finally awaken again, I feel more aware, more... present. A nurse sits beside me, her expression kind and patient. She checks my pulse, her touch gentle. "Welcome back," she says with a smile. "You've been gone for such a long time."

"Back?" I ask, my voice rasping like dry paper. "From where? I don't remember..."

"Don't worry," she reassures me. "That's normal. Your memory will return over the next few days. Just rest for now. I'll check when we can start you on fluids—you must be terribly thirsty." With that, she stands and leaves the room.

I lie back, staring up at the ceiling. It's a stormy grey, shifting and swirling as if stirred by invisible winds. The walls, too, are grey, like mist clinging to the edges of a dream. This is a strange hospital. I've never seen one painted in such oppressive colours. Aren't they usually soft pastels? Something meant to soothe, not unsettle?

The door creaks open again. A man steps inside, his presence immediately filling the room with an uneasy tension. I don't know him, but something deep within me recoils at the sight of him. I want him gone.

He speaks, his voice a dry rustle, like leaves scraping across pavement. "Good afternoon. My name is Dr. Mort." His eyes lock onto mine, cold and empty.

I stare at him, my heart pounding in my chest as I realize what I'm seeing—his face. It's not a face at all. It's a skull, grinning at me with hollow sockets where eyes should be.

The scream that tears from me is primal, pure terror incarnate. I can't stop it, can't escape it, as the world around me warps and twists, dragging me down into an abyss I can't comprehend.

Who am I? Where am I?

But the answers, if there are any, are lost in the scream, swallowed by the darkness that consumes everything.

10

Oceans Apart

Julie Gibson

"You're a brave woman, taking on this old house".

She looked at me like my mother used to—
bewilderment, tinged with scorn. She might think the house
was old, but its ancient walls had weathered the storms
better than her. Still, I let her lead me to the front door. She
scowled, "Go on, shoo, bastard birds! They're always
hanging around here"!

I didn't care; I was ready for a large drink and a nap.

The door was heavy, so we pushed it together after she
gestured, and suddenly, we met—me and the old house, just
like before. It will take some renovating, but I need a
project—a welcome distraction from what happened to
Izzy.

I caught her glaring at me, her steely blue eyes as cold as the North Sea lapping at the sand. She seemed to know more than needed to be said. "Respect the past, young lady, for it visits us often". *Yes, I thought, and mostly without invitation.* I liked being called a young lady; that is how I will always be to her, like many others.

The bay was wintry in the morning, with gulls screaming in the sky. Were they screaming at me? I wondered. The water rose to my knees as I waded in. The sea is all-consuming; I can no longer feel my legs as it enters my mouth and nose. I'm almost under. What's that noise? The screams are deafening. The gulls are in the water. I try to stop them from pecking at my flesh; cover my eyes, quick, cover my eyes! It hurts so much. I thought I was ready, but I'm not going yet.

"Are you alright, love?" I was busy coughing, so I didn't answer. The water hadn't touched me; I was dry, but I knew I had just been under.

The medication hasn't arrived.

White—that's what this old house needs—lots of white and lots of light. I couldn't face unpacking boxes, so I unpacked the pictures instead. My two girls, their excessively large, beguiling eyes and flowing brown hair, peered from beneath the plastic. Encased in their deep, white frames, they look more regal than they did in New York. As always, I hung them opposite each other, facing them so they could stare all day long. Izzy knew they needed company. Pfffft, as if any part of me thought of company. I noticed a small scratch in the glass of one. Clearly, I inherited my laser focus on faults from my mother! I will find something to remove the scratch and make it new again.

Ow! She cried, hitting the wood floor.

"Get up! What are you doing, Izzy?"

"Get back into bed; it's the middle of the night!"

She didn't get back into bed; wood keeps no secrets. I could hear her footsteps leave the room and walk down the hallway, stopping before the stairs. Then I heard no more.

The dark left me feeling even more alone and lonely than the day, but I didn't get up. The room was getting colder by the minute. I buried myself in the covers and prayed I would sleep without dreaming.

My eyes darted towards the bedroom door. There was no one there; why would there be? I scoffed at my own anxiety and grappled for my phone. It was 03:03 am; my heart was racing, but I was only half awake, just enough to feel the thud in my chest. Never too early or too late for a drink, footsteps again made the wood groan as I made my way across the hallway. I stopped at the top of the stairs as I thought Izzy had done that night. Where had she gone? I was deaf to my own footsteps as I went down the stairs; I poured a drink and went outside. The white moon pierced the black sky as I watched my breath leave me like plumes of smoke.

The frost inside the old house was a bit harder than outside. I will unpack some more boxes; it will soon be daylight.

This whimsical coastal town (my description, not Conde Nast's) is more cosmopolitan than I imagined. I have been away for so long, and I suppose everything is everywhere now. The market stalls sold olives and honey from Greece, cheeses from Spain, and Moroccan leather pouffe's straight from the souks. The music and vibrancy invigorated me. I contemplated visiting the tea shop but caved in and ordered a craft beer instead. When I say "a" craft beer, the stalls are eventually gone, and the music is only playing inside me. Dusk hardened all around, and suddenly, I could see the flashing blue lights...

"Will you be alright, love?"

"Fine, thanks...thanks for the lift.". Steadying myself. Here we were again, just me and the old house, like before. I kept peering out the makeshift white linen at the windows; the blue lights flashed outside for a while after and then, at some point, must have disappeared.

It was 03:03 am again when my head was in the sink getting rid of everything. I know I overconsume; that's just how it is. Surely, that isn't laughing! I could hear giggles coming from downstairs. What on earth...and at this hour! Undecided whether to tiptoe or race, I chose the latter, still emboldened by my excesses.

I searched every room for the laughter but couldn't find it. And then I saw my girls... Their eyes had grown even bigger, and they stood proud of the glass. I reached out my hand as if I was going to comfort them, but their eyes weren't looking at me; they were looking away as if I didn't exist. Suddenly, they reminded me of Mother, and a red mist descended. My head became a chaotic place. I reached out my hand, my index finger stroked and then pierced the eyeball. It was wet, slimy even. I didn't stop there; with three fingers in, I began scratching out the flesh. As the pupil dilated, blood began to drip. I could no longer see their bluey green hue; it was filled with red, and the veins burst open and flooded my hands. I turned and ran to the bathroom.

The medication should arrive soon.

Strong coffee is needed to tackle another day of unpacking. Before opening the boxes, I reminded myself of my purchases from yesterday, carefully taking them out of the bags. The vintage stalls had some lovely pieces. My chest stirred with an emotional swell as I took out the long black wool trench coat. Izzy had inherited one just like it, which a hand-me-down mother said was too big and old for a young girl; maybe that was true, but I had always loved it. I needed its warmth today.

Another delay to the medication, but the doctor had been in touch about the review.

The fog was so thick that the house was floating in the sky. I could just about see the gate at the end of the garden. Stepping outside, I could imagine walking from the front door straight into the ocean without even touching the grass or the sand, just as I had seen others do, not just in my head, as some liked to say. The old woman was right about the "bastard birds"; they had gathered just beyond the garden at the foot of the rocks. A dead dog was providing them with breakfast. I didn't see the dog at first, as there were so many birds. Suddenly, I felt compelled to chase them away and try to revive the dog, though a visit from the RSPCA didn't thrill me. The blue lights returned, and the familiar feeling of "*what might I have done yesterday*" drowned me from within.

"Morning love, are you okay? I was just passing and thought I would check in, as you were absolutely wasted yesterday!"

She seemed far too cheerful for a police officer. I obliged with a response; after all, she gave me a lift home: "I'm okay, thanks... well, erm...actually, I've noticed this dog over here.". She seemed the curious type and a willing hand. I couldn't believe I was putting myself in the middle of something. Whatever this something was? Charity? I zoned out but could hear, "*This dog has been scratching like hell here; I wonder if he found something... I don't like these birds*".

I wanted a walk, not a distraction, and the renovation was doing that. So I left her looking after the half-eaten dog and wandered to the beach. The mist wet my hair and face as I jumped between the rocks. Out of the corner of my eye, ever so faint, mirroring my steps, were the birds in the sky, blurred by the fog. Their path was more assured than mine; one of them lagged behind and seemed to look below, staring at me. *I want to ask for a sign to be certain of my path.* I did, and I hope they answer.

Aiming to return to the old house before dusk for once, I ran up the cliff steps. *The fog has not left here*; I mused until I looked closer. A white tent was parked on the rocks where the dead dog had been, and the blue lights were still visible. *What the hell is this? Why did I tell her about the dog? She only stopped to ask if I was okay; I needn't have said anything!* I knew she was about to speak, and so I got in first.

"What is the matter?" I didn't want to know, but they were close to the garden, which meant close to the house.

"Is this your house, love?"

"You know it is. You gave me a lift, remember?" I knew she was about to unleash a barrage of questions and instantly felt the rose that I appeared to be, bear some more of her thorns.

"Before I forget, you left this in my car yesterday. Maybe it dropped out of that coat you had. Can I come inside? I've got some questions, or if you prefer, we could do it at the station."

Yes, I preferred the station. It might seem odd to some, but the energy frequency of this old house needs to be carefully managed, as I recall. I talked more than usual today, thanks to her questions: *yes, it was my house; yes, I had just moved to the area; yes, I was decorating it; blah, blah.*

The rest of the afternoon was spent overthinking and curtain-twitching. I had come to the North East England coast for sea air and solitude and because the ocean always spoke to me. Whether Izzy and I were together or apart, the ocean washed away secrets and shame, for both of us. Returning to renovate the old house, I envisaged a blanket of quiet peppered only with the odd neighbourly 'hello' from a passerby. Now, peering at the white tent just beyond the garden, I wondered if the answers to my questions lay on that ground. I wondered if the dog or the birds had led us all to this point.

Time to pour another red tonight to go with my steak. As I tucked in, I reminisced about the birds gorging on the dead dog. Tonight, I was those birds. I like my steak rare, the reddened fluid teaming out. I tore at it, feeling every strand scrape against my teeth like shards of glass would. I looked up and caught a glimpse of my girls. I could see myself in the reflection. I let the red from the steak drip from my tongue and lips. Teasing them with it, like I had seen him do to Mother many times. Then, something piqued my attention. The girls were no longer facing each other. They had turned their backs on each other. The eyes I had scratched out were gone. *I was very, very sorry* about that. But now, look, they had turned away; their long brown hair was all I could see. No pixie face, no beguiling eyes, just hair. And it seemed all matted, not flowing and free as it had always been. *Why did I bring these from New York?* I stared into the abyss, not knowing who I was more disappointed in. Them for deserting me, or me, for thinking they would not do as others had before. Where was Izzy when all this was happening?

The medication is delayed another day, doctor, but are you still visiting her today?

I had unpacked all the boxes and put my clothes in the closet. It took all night. I had forgotten the 'new' clothes I had just bought. Grabbing them, I hung them up and remembered the note the police officer had given me. It must still be downstairs. Something inside me didn't care about some note, but something else inside me did. I listened to which voice shouted the loudest and rushed downstairs. It was an envelope, and the stamp was marked from London. I examined it. It was old and yet, somehow, also new. It hadn't been opened before unless very carefully with steam, but then again, it hadn't been opened. Peeling back the envelope, I was gentler with it than I had ever been for some reason, even more than I had been with Izzy. Inside was a postcard from Tynemouth. It looked like it was from the sixties or maybe even the fifties. I flipped it over to read the back, "*I taunt and frighten you and hurt you badly, but my love for you runs deeper than the ocean. I will return. Forever in your debt, if not in your heart. F*" Some spiders had scribbled across it in a peculiarly familiar way.

There was a knock on the door. The police officer advised that I may need to answer more questions, this time from a colleague of hers. I nodded politely and hurried back inside the old house. Officials were mingling in and out of the white tarpaulin they had erected earlier. I yearned for the answers to my questions.

It was starting to take shape—my vision for the house. The beauty of being an interior designer and being able to commission local contractors while living in New York was that the dirty work was done before I even arrived. The inventory I took for the boxes still showed a few things missing; I will chase that tomorrow. Along with a local dentist and doctor.

Walking up to the gate of the old house, I tried to ignore the mutterings of officials; they were cramping my style now! A dead fish waited for me at the front door. It had obviously dropped out of the jaws of a passing seagull; its mouth and tail were hanging loose from its body. I went to get some surgical gloves, picked it up and threw it over the cliffs. I could see one of the officials observe this behaviour as odd, but I was merely returning the fish to its rightful owner. Burying it in the ocean, I saw others take a final resting place there.

The voices were muffled, but I could hear them discussing a timeline for dismantling the white tent and removing the tape that cordoned off the area. Pressed up against the front door, I gained no clues as to what had been discovered, and so my curiosity and questions would continue.

The bath water had gone cold. I had dozed off. I woke up slumped In a heap, thankfully with my head resting over the side. I remembered finding Mother in the bath and trying to revive her as I dried every last droplet of water from my body. Cold and naked, I walked through the house, lighting all the candles—100 at last count—and scorching the air with sage. Today, I felt manic and on the verge of something I did not want to explain, not even to myself. I can't recall a time, but since the discovery of the remains near the cliffs where the dead dog was found, time has accelerated. I overheard a woman on the market this morning talking about it being an elderly lady buried there with a young girl of maybe 11 years old.

The newspapers were full of the story and the shock of finding dead bodies 'so close to home'. *Isn't it always close to someone's home*, I mused. It felt provincial and naive, like death only happens in cities and' somewhere else.

It was good news about the final boxes from New York. I trampled over the shattered glass that littered the stairs, its sharp edges puncturing the soles of my bare feet, slipping on my own blood as I went downstairs. I opened the dining room door to find the girls were no longer hanging on the wall. The frame was facing the room as if no picture existed. I didn't recall taking them down. *I was sure I only smashed the glass, as they knew I was upset. I never wanted them to turn away from me.*

The gulls were perched on the "Wonder Wheel" as if waiting for the ride to start. Although it was wintering, the park had not lost its charm on a crisp morning on Coney Island. Soon, children would devour candy and drag their parents onto the rollercoaster. Speaking of rollercoasters, the behavioural unit at the island's hospital was dealing with its usual ups and downs.

Through the window, a room in the far corner of the corridor with only a bed and a small cabinet was visible to the birds which had gathered outside. Disturbed by the clang of hospital trolleys locked in the room, she began to stir. The stench of disinfectant filled her airways as though gripped in a headlock. Motionless, the bed was like a coffin that had been left open.

The metal bars at the side to contain her.

A bird whispered through the glass: Only *the spirit is really free; the mind, too, if you master it.*

The nurse could be heard approaching. "Her medication has arrived, Doctor; I will see if she is awake.".

The little white pill was pushed into her mouth; it sat there for a moment or two, waiting for them to turn their backs so it couldn't be swallowed. Once again, she was bungled into the wheelchair; one of the porters could take her for some fresh air...and a smoke. He called his girlfriend so they could repeat an argument they had every week.

Seeing she was outside, the bird flew closer and landed beside her, its black feathers casting a shadow on the ground. It had left its flock of unkindness, which had flown by. Peering upwards, making no sound, it stood firm. The ground cracked open as the bird grew; its wings enveloped the hospital, and day transformed into night.

She had concealed the little white pill until it was no more. Yielding to the whispers of the dark, she looked up, and the bird leaned in. "You decided to return to the old house. You always preferred white. The pictures of the girls jarred against the bare stone walls, like you hoped. The police officer had to take you home, no question. You had to get the note. Such a clever girl; the writing on the postcard matched the letters contained in the trinkets from the last boxes from New York. Your father was troubled, living a half-life, but he wrote often. And your mother was willing to show you around the old house again. She looked fondly on its garden from her place near the cliffs. The ocean was always her friend, never her foe, though it may have seemed different".

The bird began to shrink, and black turned to blue, and then a burst of yellow through the white clouds. Preparing to fly, the bird stretched its wings for take-off, turning for one more goodbye. Leaning in with a whisper once more. "You must have loved your sister very much, Izzy".

11

A Tale from the Treetop: Ravens and monks

Fiona Pervez

Hold on a minute while I rip the eye out of this dead chicken.

Flying across the Vale of the Deadly Nightshade this morning, I saw Brother Peter, the cook, throwing carcasses in the pig sty. He isn't supposed to cook meat for the monks, but I saw some visitors at the abbey yesterday, so I've been on the lookout.

I know what Brother Peter does with animal entrails. I see everything that monks do from my treetop.

That wily old fox will have been foraging during the night. Still, there are a few mangled chicken heads over there, and I found one with an eye hanging out by its membrane.

Ravens have good, thick, heavy beaks; we are far superior to other birds in our family, like rooks, crows and magpies. So, pulling this eye out should be no problem. One more yank, and yes! Got it! Now I can get to the brain. Think I'll have a quick gobble to myself, then I'll go back to the roost later and point to the others with my beak. They will soon know what I'm telling them, and they'll come and feed for themselves.

So, where was I?

Oh yes, before I tell you about the evil deeds that have been going on in this holy place, I'll describe how these monks live in Furness Abbey. Well, there are some suspicious goings-on, believe me. Naturally, from my bird's eye view, I see everything. And don't think that I do not understand what I see just because I am a bird.

People underestimate ravens. They don't know that our brains are the largest of any bird species. They don't know how we have the intelligence to trick and deceive others to get what we want.

Why, just last week, I called my friend, the wolf, to come out of the woods and tear apart the old boar that fell down dead.

"How did I call the wolf?" I hear you ask.

Well, I imitated the sounds wolves make. It's a trick we ravens use to get animals to break up carcasses for us. Not a word of a lie.

Wolf was very pleased to hear me, I can tell you. It was quite a job for her to pull the old boar's limbs from its sockets and tear the hairy coat to get at the flesh underneath. But, of course, she managed it. And what did I do? Well, I just perched on a branch, sunning myself and preening my feathers until I saw some nice juicy strands of flesh hanging off the bones. Then I swooped down and tugged a beakful.

We make a good team, Wolf and I.

I'm telling you this because I want you to understand that ravens are the most capable and intelligent bird species. Not only do we communicate with each other about food sources, but we also have problem-solving abilities. You might find this difficult to believe, but Brother Peter knows it. Last week, he tied a piece of meat onto a strand of wool and hung it from a branch to see how I would get it. If a raven cannot perch on the branch, pull the wool up a little at a time and step on the loops until the meat can be reached; he is not worth a single raven-black feather. I enjoyed getting that meat and showing it to Brother Peter, who was watching. I like Brother Peter because he often feeds the birds and is kind to animals. Not like some.

This abbey is huge and very rich. The monks aren't allowed to leave the premises, so usually, they're here for life. When they're not singing and praying, they're busy growing vegetables and herbs, looking after cattle, keeping bees, making pottery, and copying the Word of the Lord. Oh yes, there's a lot of activity in an abbey. They have chapels, chapter houses, a cemetery, cloisters, stables, a buttery, a church and a kitchen. You name it, these monks have it. There's a fish pond the size of a field because the monks always have fish on Fridays.

The abbot is the chief of all the monks, and he lives in a big house, lording it over all the others. The abbot of St Mary of Furness (which is what they sometimes call Furness Abbey) is Abbot Lawrence. He is kind and devout and does not use his powerful position to indulge in a life of ease and comfort—not like some.

There's an infirmary too. I know this because I've seen the old and the sick going there. Not just monks but local villagers too. And I've seen skinny people clad in tatters going to the kitchen hoping for something to eat. Many people around here are impoverished, cold, sick and hungry. I am sure they must have a miserable life.

We Ravens fare better. Our feathers keep us warm; we stay with our families and make our homes in safe, high-up places. We can always find something to eat, even if it's just berries or dead mice or wolf pooh. It's hard in the winter, of course. But it looks harder being a human.

Ravens live long, but Furness Abbey has been here longer. The orchard is well established, the road is well trampled, and the vineyards are spreading across the hillsides.

Yes, you would think that Furness Abbey, the second richest Cistercian Abbey in the land, is set to flourish for a long time to come. I'm afraid the signs of this are not good, my friend. We ravens know a thing or two. Apart from inter-raven communication, we have been messengers since Roman times, and word gets about. A lot of humans fear us and think we bring bad luck. But humans make their own bad luck if you ask me.

The Vale of the Deadly Nightshade

Fiona Pervez

Now that you have been reliably informed about the abilities of ravens and the richness of the abbey, there is something else I must tell you.

I mentioned 'The Vale of the Deadly Nightshade', and perhaps you wonder why it is so named.

The deadly nightshade is a plant that grows around Furness Abbey. It's a distinctive plant that grows quite tall and has bell-shaped purplish flowers. It also has berries; luscious, black, shiny, juicy berries, a bit like blackberries but with smooth skin instead of bumpy seeds on the outside. The funny thing is that animals and birds eat them all the time. I like them, they're quite sweet. But if humans eat four or five of those berries, they're poisoned to death.

I know this because I saw a monk yelling at a child once (there's a school too). "Never, never pick those berries," he shouted. "If you eat them, you'll be screaming with agony, the green froth will come out of your mouth, and you'll drop down dead. Throw those berries away and wash your hands immediately."

That child ran full pelt to the stream.

One September afternoon, I was perched on my treetop, watching my mate make circles in the sky, when I noticed three monks hanging around near a clump of deadly nightshade. I noticed it because it was unusual. Monks are always busy and are not allowed to hang around in groups, passing the time of day.

It was Brother Wilfred, Brother Andrew and Brother John. I have always been suspicious of these three. I've seen them shutting the gates on the poor when the almoner wasn't there and sending villagers off without anything to eat. It's a disgrace. Ravens would never do that. And I've seen them playing Nine Men's Morris when they should be at prayer. And Brother Wilfred likes to kick the hens when he goes past. Not very monk-like behaviour, is it?

So, I took special notice of these three monks. They were talking in low voices and turning around as if to check that no one was watching them. It looked to me like a conspiracy in the making. With my beady eyes, I saw them pick poisonous berries and hide them under the folds of their greyish-white habits. It was obvious they were up to no good. Murder, probably. What else would they do with poisonous berries?

Have you ever seen pictures of monks? They wear long, woollen habits and have their hair cut in what they call a tonsure. They shave the top of their heads completely, leaving a ring of hair to remind them of Christ's crown of thorns. Oh yes, I have knowledge of the Bible. Because of our intelligence and dependability in message-bearing, ravens were the first to be sent off the ark by Noah to see if the floods were receding.

Anyway, on that September afternoon, I decided to have a little fun. I made a great cawing noise as loud as possible, and my dear old mate joined in too. We dive-bombed those three monks, swooping down, flapping our wings and dropping our lime all over their heads and habits.

Caw, Caw, Caw. Caw.Caw

Ha ha! I wish you could have seen them. They had always been superstitious of ravens, but they were positively terrified on this occasion. They started yelling and cursing, waving their arms around and bumping into each other. I managed to drop quite a lot, I can tell you. It was very satisfying to see it dripping down their necks and plastered all over their bare scalps.

I had a scary moment when my claw got caught in the woollen fibres of Brother John's habit, but I screeched, cawed, flapped, and pecked like a raven from the jaws of hell. Then I got away.

Brother John was a mess, to be sure. All the berries in his habit had squashed, and there was a big black, inky stain all over the greyish-white wool. My beak had grazed his face, and there was blood on his cheek and, of course, raven droppings all over his head. I swooped close to his face and made him stumble into a ditch. So, there was mud too. He would not slip back into the abbey buildings without being noticed.

I felt it was a good day's work and returned to my treetop quite exhausted. But I decided to be on the lookout for what they would do next.

I watched those monks very carefully.

The Murder

Fiona Pervez

People think monks and abbots are holy people who dedicate their lives to the glory of God and who fill their days with good deeds. That's the idea: to take vows of obedience, chastity, and poverty and be as good as possible. They heal the sick, feed people experiencing poverty, pray for the souls of the departed, and study the Bible.

Does it work like that? Oh no, it most certainly does not. We had an abbot some time ago, Abbot Alexander Banke, who threw people out of their homes by force and then claimed the land for himself. Once, he destroyed a complete village called Sellergarth. Of course, that was against the law, and he kept having to go to court. But he just carried on and made his very own deer park! He got mixed up between being an abbot and a king. He was very unpopular and rich, so much for the vow of poverty. He's dead now, and good riddance!

So, it was no surprise to me that Furness Abbey could be the home of the kind of people who could plot a murder. I suspected that these three monks were jealous of Abbot

Lawrence, who was saintly, devoted, and trusted everyone. Mistake. I suspected those three monks wanted everything Abbot Lawrence had, including the vast deer park.

Being a member of the most intelligent bird family, I soon learned where these brothers slept by perching on the windowsill outside the dormitory and hanging around the cloisters nearby. The monks noticed me and started talking, ignoring the vow of silence.

"That bird's back again," they said, glowering at me. "It's always hanging about. A bad omen."

I cawed and flapped, shifting my body weight from one foot to another. I was always hanging about because I had a good idea of their plot. They would pick deadly nightshade berries, squash them and add them to the wine in the communion cup. Then, the chalice would be given to the abbot, who, thinking he was taking Holy Communion, would drink it with reverence. But there would not be the blood of Christ in that chalice. There would be deadly poison.

I should think that putting poison in a holy chalice is committing sacrilege as well as murder. And the motive is clear. When poor Abbot Lawrence is dead, who will take his place? Brother Andrew, Brother John or Brother Wilfred? Whoever became abbot would take control of the abbey, not forgetting the other two. All bound together by the sin of murder.

Can you detect a flaw in this plot? Yes, you've got it. If someone drinks something and then falls down screaming in agony and then dies, poison is going to be suspected, isn't it? And then the hunt for the perpetrators would be on. And murder is a hanging offence. Not very bright, these monks.

I must have been flying further afield on the day those three picked more berries. Or perhaps they did it in the night when no one could see. Anyway, the next thing I know, Brother Edward, the infirmarian, is scurrying from the abbot's house to the infirmary and back, pointing and talking urgently. He hurried about, giving orders, collecting medicines and lifting his head to the heavens, praying to the Lord for mercy.

But all was in vain. Soon, the last sacraments were administered, the bells tolled, and a melancholy hush fell throughout the abbey.

After a little while, I saw the body of Abbot Lawrence, in his Cistercian habit, being carried from the abbot's house to the church. The monks followed, with their heads cast down, chanting prayers. Some were wiping away tears. The faithful would watch over Father Lawrence during the night in preparation for Requiem Mass and burial the next day. To lose such a pious abbot was a sad day for Our Lady of Furness. And to think that the good abbot had been poisoned by his monks!

Brothers John, Andrew, and Wilfred are very much in the background. Their faces are pale, and their eyes are shifty. They start to get very nervous. If ever men had a guilty look about them, those three did.

I tormented them by following them and hopping from ledge to wall to windowsill. Brother Wilfred got agitated and threw a stone at me.

"Get away from here, you ugly great crow," he hissed.

I was more offended by being called a crow than hurt by the stone, I can tell you. I cawed in his face and flapped my wings, making him squeal and duck his head. But I was also furious and thought about what I could do to point the blame at the rightful culprits. Brothers John, Andrew and Wilfred would not get away with such wickedness if I could help. So, do you know what I did?

I upped my game. Slyly and with the utmost care, I picked some deadly nightshade berries. But I did not eat them. I carried them individually in my beak and placed them outside the window where those wicked monks slept. After a while, there was quite a noticeable pile. Clever, don't you think? Now, anyone could see that these poisonous berries had been picked from the plant, taken a distance away, and deliberately placed where certain monks slept. A pointer. A sign. You would have to be unobservant and rather stupid not to see what *that* meant.

Brother John spotted them first. He nearly collapsed with fear when he saw that pile of berries outside his window. His face went as white as a barn owl in the dark, and his legs started to tremble. He staggered and began making noises like a donkey with the hiccups. He stamped on the berries and ground them into the grass with the heel of his sandal.

No matter, I thought. I can always get some more.

Then I watched as Brother John scurried off to find the other two. I was gratified to see he had to visit the reredorter first. The shock must have loosened his bowels somewhat. Amused, I flew to my treetop for a comfortable place to watch the goings-on below.

It wasn't long before I saw the three of them, heads huddled together, walking towards the cloisters. Then they split up. Soon, they were called to Vespers or evening prayer, and it was supper time in the refectory.

During supper time, I perched on the ledge outside the doorway. Some monks did not eat anything for fear of being poisoned. They kept giving furtive glances to each other, trying to decide who had murdered the abbot. They knew it had to be one of them.

All the monks then went to bed as usual, but the next day, guess what? Yes, three monks were missing. And there are no prizes for guessing which three.

They had gone, vanished, along with bread and cheese from the kitchen. So, as soon as the sub-prior, whose job it was to take the register, noted and recorded their absence, their guilt was confirmed.

The prior was the abbot's deputy, and he had to take over until a new abbot was appointed. That meant being responsible for the security of the monks. He also had to organize an inquest, which would decide the cause of Abbot Lawrence's death.

There didn't seem much else for me to do now that the sorry business was in the hands of the officials. But I did fly very high in the sky and saw those monks running and hiding and getting as far away from Furness Abbey as they could.

I took great pleasure in following them and suddenly flying in front of their faces when they least expected it. I got my own back on Brother Wilfred by landing on his bald head and scratching his scalp with my sharp claws.

"It's the devil that comes to haunt us in the form of a crow. He's got his evil eye on us, and we will never be free of him," he said, talking utter gibberish in his dread and his fear. I screeched my disgust.

The last time I saw them, they were heading for the woods, well away from the road. They were quarrelling amongst themselves, hungry, cold and very dirty. Their habits were torn to shreds, and their eyes were wild and desperate.

They were never caught, but I doubt they survived the winter.

This is a true story, and it is all written down in the Furness Abbey Coucher Book, a huge book with a wooden cover. It is called coucher because that is the French word for 'to sleep', and because it is so big and heavy, it always has to be laid down on a flat surface.

I bet there is nothing about ravens in the Furness Abbey Coucher Book or my part in identifying those murderous monks. But that is all right because my mate has been busy laying eggs, and we have a brood of hatchlings to feed. For now, I am content to enjoy my raven family, and I have no wish to be part of the human world and its wickedness.

12

The Shadow Man

Marjorie Dearn

Steve gazed out of the kitchen window. The view of the valley was stunning. Bathed in early evening sunshine, it had the wow factor plus. His imagination began to wander. Before the roads and railway altered the terrain, the valley must have extended to Dalton.

Jen, his wife, entered the kitchen and broke his train of thought.

"All done. Albie's bathed, in bed and waiting for his story. I'll have coffee ready when you come down."

Steve climbed the stairs two at a time. Albie was snuggled under the bedcovers, pink-cheeked and with damp curls clinging to his forehead. As always, his arms were wrapped around his teddy bear.

"OK, Albie, what is it going to be tonight? Tales from the Farmyard or the Adventures of Captain Blunder and his Pirate Crew?"

"Captain Blunder, please, Daddy."

Steve pulled the book from the bedside pile. As he thumbed through the pages to find the next story, Albie sat up in bed.

"Will the Shadowman come again tonight Daddy?"

Steve paused. "What's a Shadowman, Albie?"

"He came last night and stood there." Albie pointed to the foot of his bed.

"Albie, I think you had a dream, or maybe a car came over the top of the hill. You know how the headlights can shine through the curtains."

Albie looked doubtful but settled back on his pillow. His eyelids began drooping, and Albie was fast asleep before Steve finished the story.

Jen had brewed the coffee and was sitting with her feet curled up on the settee.

"Albie has just said an odd thing." Steve poured his coffee and sat next to Jen. "He asked if the Shadowman was coming again tonight. He said he came last night and stood at the foot of the bed."

Jen frowned. "He asked me the same question about a week ago, but I thought he'd been dreaming. Where on earth has this come from? When I take him to school on Monday, I'll have a word with his teacher. Perhaps it's something they are learning or a game they play."

On Monday morning, Miss Peterson was at the door, shepherding the infants into their classroom. Catching her eye, Jen mouthed 'Can I have a word?"

Miss Peterson nodded. She ensured all the children were settled and left her assistant to take the register.

"I'm afraid I can't leave the class, but I can keep the door open if you don't mind talking in the corridor."

As they sat on a long, low bench, Jen explained about Albie's Shadowman. "I wondered if it was something the children might have invented," she ended.

Miss Peterson shook her head. "I can assure you that there is nothing we are teaching in class, nor are there any games played that could be associated with shadows. Playtimes are always supervised so that we can pick up on these things. This seems a bit deep for children of Albie's age. This is a difficult question, but could he be worried about something?"

"No. We have asked him."

"To be honest, I didn't think so. He's a lovely child. Such a sunny nature. He mixes well with the other children and loves lessons. Mrs. Matthews, if you agree, I'll casually mention that he can always talk to me if he is worried about anything. It might be an idea if I mention to all the children that they can talk to me if they have any concerns, just in case anyone else has a Shadowman." Miss Peterson hesitated. "There is just one thing. I've noticed Albie is always lively on Mondays but seems more subdued at the end of the week." She laughed. "I guess we're all the same, ready to recharge our batteries at the weekend. Please don't worry, Mrs Matthews; I'm sure this will sort itself."

Jen felt reassured after her conversation with Miss Peterson. After collecting Albie from school, they sat at the kitchen table with a glass of milk and biscuits.

"Miss Peterson said if I was worried about anything, anything at all, I could tell her, so I did." Albie seemed unconcerned as he nibbled the icing on his biscuit.

Jen froze but managed to keep her voice steady. "And what did you talk about?"

"I told her I was worried about the tadpoles in the pond. There are millions of them, and I'm worried that they haven't got room to swim. She said they would probably take it in turn. Can I have another biscuit, please?"

Jen hugged him. "Just this once."

During the week, two of Albie's friends had 5th birthdays and, with the excitement of two parties, the Shadowman was forgotten.

Steve had worked late all week and had seen little of Jen and Albie. When Saturday dawned bright and sunny, Steve suggested they spend the day on the beach with a picnic. They built sandcastles with moats, fished for tiddlers and played in the shallow water, with Steve pulling Albie as he floated on his back. Jen thought she'd never seen the pair so happy.

That evening, Albie was almost falling asleep in the bath. He yawned as Jen carried him to his bedroom.

"He's shattered but would still like a story." Jen dropped onto the settee.

Steve pulled himself up out of his chair and stretched. The fresh air and sun were also having an effect on him. When he reached Albie's room, he was still awake.

"Would you like another pirate story, Albie?"

"Please."

Steve reached for the book.

"Will the Shadowman come again tonight?"

Steve's tiredness suddenly disappeared. "Why? Did he come again last night?"

Albie sighed and nodded. "I heard him whispering. I think he wants me to go with him."

Steve stroked Albie's head, wanting to reassure but not frighten him.

"Albie, no one is going to take you. I'll not allow it. I'll send him away with a thick ear if he ever tries to take you."

Albie smiled, clutched his teddy bear and fell asleep.

When he walked into the lounge, Jen could see he was worried,

"Oh no, not again. I'd hoped we were getting over this."

Steve sat beside her and took hold of her hand. "What if I spend tomorrow night in Albie's room? If there is anything - headlights, owls flying about, whatever, at least we'll know."

On Sunday evening, Steve had his story prepared: "Albie, I've done a silly thing. I spilt a glass of water on the bed and had cold, wet feet last night. Would you sleep in my bed tonight? You'll not have cold feet because yours won't reach the end of the bed."

Albie looked thoughtful. "Can Ted come too?"

"Course he can," Jen smiled.

The following morning, Jen woke Steve with a mug of tea. "Well?"

"I've had a perfect night's sleep. I woke up at about 3.30ish and looked around. Nothing. Then I fell asleep again."

Albie returned to his bedroom, and the week progressed as normal. Jen had promised to visit her neighbour, Mrs Allen, and wondered if she might know of any stories, folklore, or anything that concerned the valley that Albie may have overheard. She admitted to herself that she was clutching at straws.

As always, Mrs Allen was pleased to see her and happily accepted the tin of Jen's biscuits. A pot of tea was brewed, and they settled in the lounge.

"You've lived here for a long time, haven't you?" Jen began.

"Yes, dear. Three generations of my family have lived in this house."

"Then you'll know a lot about the history of the area and the people who lived in our house."

"Yes, yes, I do. The Banks lived there before you. Must have lived there thirty years or more. He worked at the Shipyard. They had four daughters. Two live in Canada, one lives in Surrey and one in Kent. They moved south to be near their grandchildren. Now before them it was the Burlingtons. No children, but they always kept Labradors. Must have been there twenty years. Before them, it was the

Sawyers. Lovely family." She sighed and shook her head. "Such a tragedy."

"What was so tragic?" asked Jen quickly before Mrs. Allen could continue.

"Their son disappeared one night. He was only five years old. He was never found. Suspicion fell on the family, but no one was ever charged. They worshipped that boy. All of them."

Jen's brain began buzzing. She needed to know more about this family.

"If you are interested in the history of this area, and your house in particular, why not go to the Archives at Barrow Library? The staff are so helpful."

Jen spent most of Thursday in the Archives, poring through yearbooks and records, until eventually she discovered an account of Edgar Sawyer's disappearance. The local newspaper had covered the story for weeks. Then, one article caught her eye. 'Has History Repeated Itself?' ran the headline. The story referred to another five-year-old boy, James Culpepper, who had disappeared almost 60 years previously. Jen needed to pick up Albie from school, and time was running short. She quickly jotted down the details she needed and thanked the staff.

After Albie was settled for the night, Jen and Steve sat with her notes.

"This sounds completely mad, but there is a pattern here. Both boys lived in this house and may have even slept in the same room as Albie. There's something else. Have you noticed Albie always asks on Saturdays if the Shadowman will come back again - he sees him on Fridays!"

"I think you are on to something here, Jen. Right, I'll spend tomorrow night in Albie's room. I promise we will get to the bottom of this."

"You haven't spilt water again, have you, Daddy? " Albie asked when he was told he would have to spend another night with Jen.

Steve looked sheepish. "I must be getting clumsy in my old age Albs."

Albie looked at Jen and rolled his eyes.

Steve glanced out of the window. A clear sky, almost a full moon, no breeze to stir the trees. Although his mind was troubled, he quickly fell into a deep sleep. He awoke when the room was still in darkness and lay for a moment without moving. Curious to know the time, he reached for his mobile phone. The air was icy cold, cold enough for him almost to lose his grip on the phone. His gaze wandered to the foot of the bed. A large, dark, human form, devoid of facial features, towered over him. He gasped aloud and grabbed the bedclothes. As he did, the form shook violently, angry at seeing Steve. He struggled to get out of bed but couldn't move. There was pressure on his chest. He was fighting to breathe. Some force was holding him down, and he knew it was evil. He tried to shout but could make no sound nor take his eyes off the figure. He felt as though his life was being slowly sucked from him, but Albie was safe.

Albie! The thought of his son gave Steve the impetus he needed. He managed to roll out of the bed, then, pushing himself up onto his hands and knees, he crawled slowly towards the door. Energy was draining from him, but with one last effort, he fell through the doorway onto the landing. He was shivering. With cold or fright, he neither knew nor cared. Although his legs would hardly support him, he stumbled down the stairs, clinging to the bannister. When Jen walked into the kitchen, he was trying to make a hot drink. She was horrified by the sight of him. His hands were shaking so violently that he couldn't grasp the tap.

Jen wrapped her arms around him and led him into the lounge, putting a blanket over his shoulders. "Can you tell me?" she asked gently.

He gave her a halting account of what had happened. "Jen, I've never experienced anything like it. The room was filled with evil. It was icy cold and horrifying. That figure!" He shuddered. "I thought I was going to die."

Jen made them both mugs of hot, sweet tea. "I have something I need to tell you. I couldn't sleep, so I decided to do more research on my laptop. Both the boys who disappeared were five years old. Both disappeared on a Friday night. I've checked the dates, and Albie will be five years old in three weeks. Steve, there is something else. This valley is called the Vale of the Deadly Nightshade, named after the plant that grows here. But there is another meaning of 'shade'. It can also mean ghost, spirit, or phantom. Don't you see? Vale of the Deadly Nightshade could also be Vale of the Deadly Night Spirit - Vale of the Deadly Night Phantom."

Acknowledgements

First and foremost, I want to express my heartfelt thanks to everyone who made the publication of this book possible.

To my dear friend and talented artist, Claire Gardner, a special thank you for sharing your incredible art project with me. The moment I saw your magnificent painting of 'Merlin' the raven, I was captivated. It sparked the creative process that brought this book to life. When I shared your image with my fellow authors, they were equally inspired, eager to craft their stories around it.

A huge thank you to my fellow authors—Laura Billingham, Jo A. Ripley, Fiona Macintosh Pervez, F. Taylor, Julie Gibson, Pamela Edwards, Dorothy King, Margaret Martindale, and Marjorie Dearn—whose unique and original stories have made this collection truly special. Your collaboration and contributions have been invaluable.

To our many supporters, I especially want to acknowledge Amanda France and Julie Woodhams, who provided unwavering encouragement, insightful feedback, and brilliant ideas in the early stages. Your support meant the world to me.

To the ARC (Advanced Reading Copy) team: Pam G., Sharon S., Carla Marie S., Claire G., Martin H., Catherine T., Amanda F., Tracy B., Vicky Clarke B., Julie W., Rebecca K., Chris W., Sharon D., Sarah R., Maureen C., Emma Leon-P., Gill M., Jane H., Janet W., Sheila M.—your honest feedback and thoughtful reviews have been absolutely priceless.

Finally, my deepest gratitude to my publisher, The Book Chief, and to Sharon Brown and her exceptional team. Your talent, guidance, and unwavering support throughout this process have been truly remarkable.

About the Authors

Lead Author - Ellie LaCrosse

Ellie LaCrosse has enjoyed a diverse professional career before moving to Cumbria to embrace a more creative and bohemian lifestyle. She has self-published several books on Amazon, including poetry collections and a memoir, as well as various digital assets. Ellie enjoys experimenting with different genres to continually hone her writing craft.

You can connect with her on Facebook: Ellie LaCrosse - Author.

Julie Gibson

Julie Gibson is an explorer and adventurer currently residing by the sea in North East England. With a wide range of pursuits that include technology, property, healthcare, and art, Julie is driven by a strong desire to improve life for everyone. Having previously had poems published, Julie is now venturing into writing both non-fiction and fiction, including stories, novels, and plays.

Fiona Pervez

Fiona Pervez was born in Cumbria and has a deep love for exploring the Lake District and researching local history. Her stories are set in Cumbria, grounded in local myths, traditions, and historical events, with elements of fantasy and the supernatural woven throughout. Fiona also collaborates with a textile art group to create multi-media work, including creative writing, which is often exhibited across the county. Her favourite creative pursuit is discovering intriguing pieces of history and building captivating stories around them.

Margaret Martindale

Margaret Martindale's upcoming publication marks her first foray into the world of published writing. Her storytelling journey began with her children, as she crafted imaginative tales about the creatures and plants they encountered on their walks. This tradition continued with her grandchildren. Encouraged by a friend, she later joined a creative writing class, where she honed her skills. Margaret enjoys reading mystery and sci-fi, genres that continue to inspire her storytelling.

Laura Billingham

Laura is an author and editor living in the Peak District, UK. Mother to two grown-up daughters and granny to one (with another due in June), she styles herself as the Word Witch and spends her days enmeshed in the written word—finally living the dream she had as a young woman.

Dorothy King

Dorothy King is married with three children and a retired self-employed cake maker. Despite the challenges of dyslexia, she developed a deep love for reading after mastering it, starting with her first book at the age of nine. Dorothy and her family grow most of their own vegetables and fruit on their allotment, and in her spare time, she enjoys swimming and playing darts, even if not very well. A highlight of her week is attending a friendly and constructive writing group, where she continues to develop her passion for storytelling.

Pamela Edwards

Pam Edwards is a successful Business Creation & Development Strategist, Consultant, and Speaker Trainer based in Nottingham, UK. With a career focused on helping independent business owners, Pam now works with clients to build strong foundations and frameworks for long-term business success. While she has primarily written about business topics, this marks her first venture into a different genre. Pam has previously contributed to *The Small Business Owners Handbook* and *The Secrets of 99 Successful Women*.

Jo A. Ripley

Jo Ripley, based in Cumbria, is a spiritual coach and moon magic mentor with several self-published non-fiction works. This is her first short story in the fiction realm, exploring the supernatural—an area she is intimately familiar with as a psychic-medium. Jo has long been passionate about writing, having previously created poetry and songs, and was featured in an anthology during her teenage years.

Marjorie Dearn

Marjorie Dearn has had a lifelong love of books, which played a significant role in her life from an early age. After taking early retirement, she enrolled in a night school creative writing class and quickly became hooked. Marjorie continues to nurture her passion by meeting weekly with fellow creative writers at a local café in her Cumbrian town.

And finally…

F. Taylor

F. Taylor, born and raised in Birmingham, developed a deep love for literature from a young age. After pursuing that passion academically, Taylor earned a degree in English Literature from Bangor University. Despite a keen interest in storytelling and writing, F. Taylor prefers to remain anonymous, allowing the work to speak for itself rather than seeking personal recognition.

Printed in Great Britain
by Amazon